HOLLOW HOUSE

MK AHEARN

To my FBI agent watching, this is what the research was for and I hope it makes you blush.

TRIGGER WARNINGS

This book contains the following potentially triggering content. Please take care of yourself and proceed with caution with this in mind.

Sexually explicit content, intercourse next to a dead body, fear play, knife play, dubious consent, swearing, blood , drugging , secret society , rituals/cult like behavior, stabbing, ghosts, voyeurism , assault, sexual harassment, and use of sex toys.

A Note from the Author

Please keep in mind that this is a novella. It is meant to be a short and quick read. This is not a full length novel and there are not plans to turn it into one. Thank you for giving this dark romance novella a chance!

PLAYLIST

I WRITE SINS NOT TRAGEDIES
PANIC AT THE DISCO

MASQUERADE OF THE GHOSTS
DEREK FIECHTER AND BRANDON FIECHTER

DANCE FOR ME WALLIS
ABEL KORZENIOWSKI

DANCE, DANCE
FALL OUT BOY

THE SUMMONING
SLEEP TOKEN

DARK ARIA
SAWANO HIROYUKI

ZOMBIE
THE CRANBERRIES

WELCOME TO

HOLLOW HOUSE

CHAPTER 1

I typed aggressively at my computer in my little cubicle. The edits for the article I'd been working on were due before close of business.

The headline, *Pumpkin Spice Season*, felt too cliché. I could do better.

It was that time of year again. Already, the air had turned crisp, and I found myself breaking out my sweaters. Today's was black with tiny skulls on it, one I knew my boss would hate.

Fuck his opinion. Darren lost any semblance of respect the second I realized what a douche he was, a creep with a habit of spending far too long looking at my ass.

The thought completely distracted me from the work in front of me. I needed a reset. I stood from my tiny desk chair, one that made my back ache after sitting at it all day.

The kitchen wasn't far from where I sat, and I knew someone else had brought in apple cider donuts for the office. A sweet treat had to be enough to get me back on track. Voices hit me as I reached the doorway…

Fuck.

It was far too late to turn around. I already stepped inside and was met with side glances from two women chatting.

"Do you really think you'll be invited this year…" one trailed off.

I tried not to look like I was listening as I found the box of donuts on a nearby table. A pile of napkins sat beside it, and I used one to carry my treat.

"Of course. I did everything I could. Fucked every wealthy man possible in this small town, built a bigger social media presence. Shit, if I don't catch their eye, no one will," she said firmly.

"Yeah but Hollow House is nearly impossible to get in to. No one even knows what an invite looks like."

"Well, once I'm invited, Darren will promote me. He was practically salivating at the idea of an exclusive inside look."

I rolled my eyes and turned away from them. I didn't have time to be distracted by parties or whims. I had my sights set on a bigger ideal. I wanted to get out of the small town and move to a big city.

Dani from Marketing, however, had started a blogging page online and grew a rather large audience over the past year. It'd been great for the magazine we worked at, practically free advertising. But Halloween was only a day away, and that left almost no time at all for her to find an invite to Hollow House.

Everyone wanted an invite, but nearly no one received one. Most of the rumors surrounding what happened within were just that: rumors, started by people with nothing better to do and all the time in the world.

A full pot of coffee sat freshly brewed on the counter, and as much as I wanted to hurry back to my work, I knew caffeine could do me some good.

I grabbed one of the paper cups from next to the machine and poured some inside. The fridge had multiple options for creamer, and I settled on a pumpkin pie flavored one. The coffee lightened as I poured a splash in, and Dani and the other woman droned on.

I moved to leave the kitchen and stumbled, splashing hot coffee on myself. My foot hit something solid, and I turned to find the two women snickering as Dani pulled her foot back in.

"Shit," I muttered, realizing I had coffee on myself.

What were we, fucking petty teenagers? Some people needed to grow up. It wasn't the first time I found myself the target of their cruelty.

I opened my mouth but thought better of it, leaving the kitchen silently instead. Sooner or later, they'd grow bored of me, realize they peaked in high school, and the real world wouldn't tolerate their shit.

When I returned to my cubicle, I tried to refocus on naming the article I'd created.

"Sloane Hill!" my boss' pestering voice called from his office.

Before I could make my way from my cubicle to his door, his head poked out. The man locked eyes with me, and I sighed.

Whatever he wanted could wait, but he'd never allow it. In his mind, everything he wanted was an emergency, more important than the piece I had pulled up to edit.

I walked slowly over to his office and dreaded it the moment his door shut behind us. His hand found its way to my shoulder, and I cringed from his touch.

"Have a seat," he said, his voice like nails on a chalkboard.

Three years, I put up with it. Three years, I had worked tirelessly to climb my way up the ranks of the local magazine I worked for. He was a dick, always spending far too long with the younger women who worked beneath him, the lingering touches, the excuses for time alone. The rumors that floated through the halls should have been enough to have him out of a job, but that would require someone believing them.

I kept my head down, did my work, and steered clear of him when I could. All I needed was enough in my portfolio to apply to the bigger magazines, my ticket out of this small town.

Right now, though, I was stuck in the cheap office chair on the opposite side of his desk, uncomfortably shifting beneath his glare. I fidgeted with my V-neck sweater, trying to shift it to deter his wandering eyes, but they immediately dropped to my thighs exposed by the black miniskirt I wore. I cursed under my breath, wishing I was bundled up more.

"It's time for your performance review," he said, folding his hands on his desk.

"It's October?" I questioned. "Isn't that in another two months?"

"I'm doing an impromptu one for you," he said with a shrug.

"Is that even legal?" I muttered.

"First part of your review: lacks respect for authority. You need to get a grip on this attitude you carry around the office."

My hands clenched into firsts beside me, my ass

sliding to the edge of the seat, ready to storm out. I didn't have to put up with this insanity.

"Secondly, your performance lately has been lackluster," he added.

"Excuse me?" I gritted out through clenched teeth.

"Lackluster," he clicked, exaggerating with his tongue.

I cringed into the seat, wishing I could bleach my mind. Fucking creep.

"I complete all my work on time, I've taken on extra projects, and I have had zero negative feedback," I started.

"You play it safe," he said with another shrug. "There's nothing spectacular about that."

I almost growled, the low noise forming deep in my throat. The man who sat on his ass all day and harassed women for fun was critiquing my work product?

Fuck, no.

"We're done here," I said firmly as I stood.

"Sit," he ordered, his tone impatient.

I stared him down, my skin on fire at the demand.

I didn't sit, but I didn't leave.

"One call to management, and you're gone," he hissed. "Don't be an ungrateful bitch. I'm trying to help you."

The smug smile on his face made me want to

punch him square in the middle of it. Instead, I clenched my fists, digging my nails into my palms. A single deep breath was enough for me to realize he'd follow through on the threat. The turnover in our department was proof enough.

"What do you want me to do?" I gritted out, still standing.

"Be a bit more interesting," he suggested.

"How do you expect me to do that?"

He leaned back in his chair, running a hand through his short brown hair. The movement caused his shirt to rise and stomach to poke out a bit from the bottom. He raised a brow at me, and it took seconds of me staring blankly at him to realize what he was suggesting.

He couldn't be serious…

"The most successful women here do what it takes to get to the top," he said, his hand moving toward his zipper.

"I'm not—" I started.

"The miniskirts you wear, the slutty pink strands in that long, dark hair," he said, his gaze turning predatory. "You've been practically begging me to notice."

"Excuse me?" I asked, anger rising deep in my chest.

No fucking way. I wouldn't blow the guy to keep my position.

"Well, you have my attention now, Sloane. The question is, will you do what it takes to stay here?"

Creative new expletives raced through my mind, and I sorted through which I wanted to use first. Was this how the women here moved their way up? What a fucking sick and twisted cruelty!

Did Dani get promoted like this? Was Hollow House really her ticket to another promotion—

I stopped the thought there, a new idea forming.

"I'll write about Hollow House," I spat out before I could stop.

"Dani is—" he started.

"Incapable of writing and still hasn't received an invite," I pointed out, folding my arms.

The bitch deserved a bit of karma and I deserved the chance to rid myself of the toxic workplace I'd called a job for three years. They all deserved each other at this point.

Darren folded his hands in his lap, no longer reaching for his zipper. His attention fully settled on me.

For a moment, I thought maybe I did screw myself. Maybe quitting would've been easier. At least then, I could leave on my own terms without being kicked to the curb.

"Fine," Darren answered. "If you get me an inside

scoop on Hollow House, you can have the promotion I know you've been waiting for."

Not quite what I was working for, but it definitely would help my plan to get out.

"I expect the article in my inbox on November 1."

An impossible turnaround, of course.

"Fine," I said flatly.

I turned to walk out, not willing to waste time, ready to get to work on the impossible task I just assigned myself.

"Good fucking luck," Darren chuckled on my way out.

CHAPTER 2

I left work immediately.

There was less than a day until Halloween, and now, I was utterly fucked. What was I thinking? There was only a single place I could think to start, and I sighed knowing what it would cost me.

The shop was only a couple of blocks away, and a tiny bell rang when I pushed the door open. Everything from vibrators to lingerie lined the walls, and I found myself pausing to stare at a few items.

"Sloane!" Felix called out from behind the register, pulling my attention away.

I waved and hurried over to my best friend. Felix and I had known each other since kindergarten. He worked at the shop to support his dreams of becoming an author. We'd both loved writing since we were little, just in different ways. He created stories, whimsical worlds to escape into, and I reported on this world, wrote what I saw and experienced.

Luckily, he also had his partner Jeremy to support those dreams. Working at the shop gave him the flexibility to still have time for writing while Jeremy's income helped balance the bills.

They were the perfect pair.

"You've starved me of my next chapter, so I've come to demand it," I joked.

Felix sent me the chapters he wrote one at a time for feedback. His latest work was going to be an instant bestseller. This one would be the big break for him, I knew.

He threw his hands up dramatically. "I've hit a wall," he groaned. "I can't decide where I want things to go next."

"Maybe you need a change of scenery," I suggested, seizing the opportunity. "Happy hour? We could get drinks and bounce ideas back and forth."

Felix's eyes widened, and he dropped the fuzzy handcuffs he had been ringing up for a pick up order.

"I'm sorry, did I hear that right?" he said, leaning on the counter.

"What?" I questioned.

"Sloane," he answered accusingly, "you deny every invite to happy hour I text your way."

"I don't—" I started, but I stopped, realizing he was correct. "Okay, fine, but I've had a change of heart."

"What do you want?" he asked and folded his arms, his back straight. He raised a brow, waiting for my answer.

"Do I have to want something to grab a drink with my best friend?" I tried.

He raised both brows expectantly, and I sighed.

"Fine. I need to figure out a way to get an invite to Hollow House before tomorrow," I admitted.

He held up his hands to stop me from elaborating as his eyes widened even more. "This shop has ears. Drinks it is," he said, a bit quieter.

"Drinks at Val's?" I asked.

He nodded—he couldn't say no to the small bar nearby, one of our favorite spots in town.

"Hey, Jack," he called out.

"Yeah?" a friendly voice called out from a few aisles away.

"I'm heading out for the night, but I'll be back early tomorrow to prepare everything for Halloween!"

"See you tomorrow," Jack called back without question.

The walk outside was refreshing, the crisp air a reprieve from the thick sweater I wore. Felix rambled about the ideas floating in his head for his book, and I listened, soaking in every second with my friend. Even if I avoided these outings, it never meant I didn't appreciate seeing him.

It was a constant war inside my own head.

The second we arrived at Val's, I relaxed. It was a staple in the town of Dresel. In addition to the small diner down the street and the old library in the center of town, it was one of the longer-standing businesses in the town.

My own parents had frequented the place as teenagers. When the owners died, their kids took over running the place, and the spirit of the bar remained well and alive.

We took a seat in a booth, and a waitress immediately placed waters and a drink menu in front of us. I recognized her—she'd been working there for years. Felix gave her a warm smile and ordered a drink without needing the menu.

My eyes glazed over the multiple options and settled eventually on a margarita.

"It's been weeks since we've had time to hang out like this," Felix said after our drinks arrived.

"Yeah, we should do this more often," I agreed.

The pointed look I received sent guilt through me. I knew I'd been relatively unavailable recently, but had it been that bad?

"That would require you to not work all day, every day," Felix answered.

Maybe I was that bad. "It's going to pay off," I promised, fidgeting with my drink glass.

"I know you want to get out of here, but pouring everything into that place isn't it. Didn't you say your boss is a dick? Do you really think he'll help you get there?"

The words stung, but I knew he meant well. He was the one friend I trusted to always be honest with me.

"I'm working on something else, something that truly could be a big break," I admitted.

"And are you going to share what that is?" he asked.

"Yes, but another drink first," I replied, not quite ready to share my insane plan. Fuck, I should've just asked for the tequila straight.

We made our way through our drinks and on to our seconds. I opted for the strawberry margarita instead of mango on our second round. After a large gulp, I let out a deep sigh before readying myself for the conversation I knew I had to have.

"So, Hollow House," I started.

He rolled his eyes, taking a sip from his drink.

"You provide all the sex toys for the party, right?" I guessed.

He glanced around like the patrons at the bar might

overhear us, even through the loud music providing a bit of a barrier.

"Yes," he answered.

"Which is why you didn't want to discuss it at the shop?" I guessed.

"Do you know how many people would come looking for an invite to Hollow House if they knew?" he said dramatically. "We'd get nothing done. Do you know how many Hollow House followers we'd have hanging out at the shop year round? Would it be good for sales? Maybe. But we'd likely lose our top client, and it wouldn't be worth it."

"But people have to realize you're the only shop in town that sells what Hollow House would need to host a party like that," I said, not understanding how more had not come to that conclusion.

"Not when Jack complains year round that they don't," Felix said and smiled.

"What?"

"People have assumed. We just made it very clear they assumed wrong. Any work for Hollow House we do before and after hours. On Halloween, we deliver the items they need extremely early in the morning," he explained.

"Which is why you'll be back early tomorrow to help?" I guessed.

"Exactly," he confirmed. "Why are you even asking?"

"Because I need to find a way in tomorrow," I stated, like I hadn't just said the most absurd thing I could.

Felix's jaw dropped, and he set down his drink. "You can't be serious, Sloane," he said. A nervous laugh escaped his lips, watching and waiting for me to take it all back.

"Completely serious," I stated. "That's my way out. An article on Hollow House, the place the wealthiest and most influential people spend their Halloween. I would be the first to share the story from the inside."

He shook his head, his hand now on his forehead in distress. His mouth kept opening like he was going to say something, but he stopped.

"So can you get me access to Hollow House?" I asked.

"No can do," he stated.

Shit.

"Felix—" I started.

"Nuh uh, don't Felix me," he said. "I never suggested I could. I told you I could share what I knew, and I did."

I glared at him, but after only a second, I backed down. If Felix could've helped me, I knew he would've. Never once had he turned his back on me. He was my most reliable friend, and if he didn't have a way, that was that.

"Now, are you going to go over there and finally talk to that guy, or do I have to drag you?" he said, trying to lighten the mood and change the subject.

"What guy?" I asked.

"The one who's been staring at you this whole time," he answered. "Don't tell me you didn't notice?"

I shrugged. There were plenty of men seated at the bar only feet from our booth, but I hadn't paid much attention to them. I turned around, scanning for whoever he was referring to.

"Who?" I asked, turning back after seeing no one even glance slightly in our direction.

He poked his head around me, and his brows pulled together. "I swear…" He stood slightly to get a better angle, almost completely leaving his seat. "He must've left," he said, disappointed.

I looked back one more time just to be sure. A new feeling crept in, like I was being watched, but not a single patron at the bar met my gaze. The hairs on my arm stood up like a warning.

"Sloane…" Felix said, waving a hand in front of my face.

"What?" I asked, startled back into reality.

"I asked if you wanted another drink," he said, a brow quirking.

"I'm alright. I really should get going," I said with a small sigh.

My one sliver of hope was extinguished. It wasn't Felix's fault—I asked the impossible of him, but I couldn't help that small ember of disappointment from taking root.

"Want me to call you a ride?" he offered.

"No thanks," I said with a weak smile. "I'm going to walk home."

"Are you sure?" he asked, giving me a look of hesitation.

"Yes. It's barely sunset, and I'll text you the second I'm home, I promise," I assured him.

"Fine," he sighed, knowing arguing was useless. "You're lucky I have your location." He held up his phone and tapped it.

"No one's going to kidnap me, I promise," I laughed.

"You're right. If they did, they'd return you in seconds. Far too insufferable," he teased and rolled his eyes dramatically.

"Fuck off," I laughed, standing and holding out an arm to him.

He linked his own around mine as we walked out. I missed the days when it was far easier to spend nights like this, when there weren't responsibilities constantly weighing on me and holding my attention.

"We should do this again soon," I said.

"I'm sorry, did Sloane Hill just admit happy hour is actually a good time?" He gasped.

I teasingly pushed him away. "I will never admit that."

CHAPTER 3

The walk home started peacefully enough.

I crossed my arms tightly across my body, the night providing a cool breeze and taking any remaining warmth with it.

From the road I was on, there wasn't much blocking the view just beyond the small town. The one house beyond the outskirts sat on a hill, making it an easy sight to see. Its large presence remained year round.

The vague lighting of the gate to Hollow House glowed in the distance. The gothic mansion sat on a hill just outside town, and I could just see the start of the property.

Its eerie presence was like a shadow watching over everyone.

No one knew much about it, but everyone knew it was there.

When I was a child, we would bike out there just to catch a peek inside. We never saw much. Instead, we told stories about the things that happened in that house and tried to scare each other.

We were far from knowing the truth.

It wasn't until I was far older that the rumors of the party of desires started circulating. There wasn't a specific person who could point toward it being true, but each Halloween, the property lit up. Cars dropped guests off in the big half circle driveway, and the entire house remained completely alive until morning.

Then, the rest of the year, it was vacant besides the workers who took care of the property. Never once had I seen the person who owned the house. No one even knew their name.

A shiver ran down my spine, the cool breeze picking up and rustling leaves that had fallen on the sidewalk.

Only a few blocks from my house, movement to my left caught my eye, a blur I could barely make out down the alley I passed. I tried to take another step but froze, a shadow moving in my peripheral.

The hairs on the back of my neck rose, and I turned fully to face the alley. Part of me was afraid I'd find someone waiting for me. Maybe I should've had Felix walk me.

My eyes glanced down the alley, my heart pounding

in my chest, but there was nothing. No person or animal sat in the dark, only a trash bin and a few abandoned boxes outside the back door of a restaurant.

I blinked a few more times just to be completely sure. The stress of the job was getting to me. I moved on, afraid to linger much longer. It was growing pitch black out the more time I took to get back home.

My small yellow house sat on the corner of the block. The neighbors were returning home with their children for the night, and I gave a wave as I passed their driveway. It was peaceful in this section of town.

Mail poked out of the mailbox beside my front door. I emptied it, the metal clinking as the top flap shut. The mail shuffled in my hands, and I tried to maneuver finding my key while not dropping it. I pulled it out of my purse while managing to balance everything I held.

The door to my tiny house unlocked seconds after I stuck the key in, and I quickly shut and locked it behind me as I slipped inside, unable to shake the eerie feeling.

Silence was thick in the air, and I hung up my keys and purse on the little hooks next to the door. I had no pets or partner, no one waiting for me to get home.

A small thud sounded down the hall, and I dropped the mail. Instinctively, my eyes looked for the nearest weapon. The only thing I could find was a an old umbrella propped in the corner by the door. It would have to do.

I picked it up and slowly shuffled down the hall, trying to make as little noise as possible. The sound came from the kitchen straight ahead of me.

I couldn't see anyone, but the narrow hall only showed me a sliver of the space. My heart pounded, and the more sensical side of me started to wonder if I should've called the authorities.

And say what? *I heard a noise. I thought I saw a shadowy figure down an alley.* That was a sure way to have myself questioned, my sanity slipping.

I shook my head.

It was probably nothing. Exhaustion and a tough day, that was all.

I poked my head around the corner, my breath catching in my throat.

Items sat on the island counter in the middle of my kitchen. The red in the middle left me breathless as I approached, my heart still pounding.

The rose sat perfectly placed in the middle of the counter, and I reached out to pick it up. A note sat underneath the flower, and I noticed my name written in cursive on the outside. A mask sat to the side.

My hand trembled, setting the flower down and lifting the note. This wasn't in my house when I left for work, which meant someone had been inside.

Were they still?

The feeling of being watched crept back in, and my entire body trembled. My phone weighed heavy in my pocket, and the temptation to call someone grew. The tiny note remained firmly in my grasp.

My head whipped around, searching for someone, anyone, inside my home. I looked for whoever left it, wondering if they watched while I decided what to do. The black paper with white writing didn't look threatening. If someone was watching and waiting for me to open it…

The choice was simple.

Pick up the phone and call the authorities before it was too late or open the note.

I knew what I should do, what any rational person would do.

But—

I opened the note before I could think it through. Inside was a card, the outline of a rose drawn on the left and three words written on the right. The writing was more like a rose gold engraving into the black paper.

"Answer the call."

My heart stopped, the pounding gone, breathing no longer possible. I dropped the note quietly back on the island. My hands rose to my chest, clawing at it, begging myself to take a breath. I tried and forced myself to take in straggling gasps of air. After a few minutes, I managed something resembling ragged breathing.

I forced myself to pick up the mask. I knew what the invite was.

People would give anything to find those three words addressed to them. Only hours, before I had thought the same, but now, I stood in my kitchen trembling in fear.

What had I done?

I held the mask up to my face. The black material was adorned with gold. As I held it up, movement outside my kitchen window had me dropping it just as quickly. I ran to the back door and scanned the small, fenced in yard.

There was nothing there at first glance, but with the sun set, could I be sure of that? Shadows took up almost every corner of the yard. An extensive garden and a couple of trees throughout the space provided the perfect coverage.

I opened the back sliding door and stepped outside. Either adrenaline or stupidity drove me out the door. What was I going to do if someone was there? I had no protection beyond my two bare hands.

A snapping twig startled me, and I glanced in the

direction of the sound. My feet slowly moved down the two concrete steps into the grass. Little blades of the plush grass rubbed my ankles and sent shivers up my legs.

I stood there for another moment, my heart practically in my throat by that point. The wind blew, rustling the trees, but beyond that, I heard nothing.

I backed slowly toward the door, keeping my eyes on the yard. Nothing jumped out at me as out of place. There was something there, though. I couldn't explain it, the horrifying feeling that another presence sat in the shadows. My heart raced, but I found my trembling had stopped. If whoever was there hadn't hurt me yet, I didn't think they would now.

What did they want with me?

Was the invite to Hollow House my answer?

After a couple minutes of standing frozen with one foot in the door, I shut the slider door, giving up on seeing anything.

Instead, I turned my attention back to the invite I dropped. I picked it up again, turning it over and over in my hands. Was this even real, or was it a cruel joke?

Things couldn't be that easy, right?

It begged the question: what did they want with me? Had my single day of poking around caught their attention? Felix had warned me the shop had ears.

He was usually right.

Maybe whatever took place at the pleasure house was something they didn't want a journalist poking into. That fueled me even further to chase the article. Once I set my sights on a story, nothing stood in my way.

CHAPTER 4

My eyes had been set on her since I first saw her in town.

That little bar, Val's.

That was when I knew I had to make her mine.

Each year was the same. I found someone to entertain me through the night. There were plenty of woman capable and willing who came to Hollow House, but no one had truly satiated me. My appetite only grew each year.

I needed the one who would stay forever.

The second I saw her long, brown hair trailing down her back, pink streaks mixed in, heard the way she laughed as the waitress handed her a drink, I knew she was the one.

I had eyes and ears everywhere.

Everyone wanted an invite to Hollow House. Most

never received it. This was my game, my muse, and I wouldn't share it with just anyone.

Only those with potential were invited, those like me, whom the world cast aside and doubted. Now look at us.

I found the perfect prey to welcome into our midst.

It only took twenty minutes of digging to find out who she was.

I sat at the bar in the quaint little town center and researched until I had everything I needed. Her friend kept glancing my direction, but I didn't mind. I would be gone before she noticed.

I finished my glass of whiskey in a single gulp and left the waitress a fifty dollar tip. It was the least I could do to give back to the small town that accepted my depravity. They craved it, coveted it.

Who was I to deny them?

CHAPTER 5

The black dress hugged my curves down to my midthigh. I debated wearing the black lace tights I recently bought, torn between it being too much or not. The note gave no indication of a dress code, but I knew what the rumors said.

I decided not to wear them.

The party was filled with the wealthiest, all pulled in by one man himself: the man who owned the large estate sitting just outside of town. No one knew his name or when he came to town, but most agreed he was some form of millionaire. An investor, maybe?

Mentally, I added it to the list of things I wished to gain from the party. I was going with a purpose. This article would pull me out of the small town I was stuck in and allow me the freedom I sought.

A knock at the door abruptly pulled me from the thought.

My heart nearly stopped, and I knocked over the glass of wine I poured myself earlier in the night for courage. A towel sat slung over on my vanity chair, and I grabbed it, tossing it over the spill. Thankfully, it was just white wine. Red would've been a bitch to clean up.

I hurried down my stairs to the front door, throwing it open. Felix didn't wait for an invite, walking in right past me. He went straight for the steps, and I followed, shutting the door.

By the time we made it back to my room, I felt out of breath as the adrenaline finally settled. My nerves crept back in about the party, and one look to my friend told me he knew.

"You're seriously doing this?" he asked, eyeing me. "Sloane, who never wants to grab drinks and works all day, every day, is going to Hollow House?"

I nodded. "Please don't try to talk me out of it," I started, sure that if he did, I would instantly cave.

"Oh, I won't. I think you desperately need to get laid," he said, shaking his head at me. "Wear the slutty heels." He point to the corner, where my black heels I reserved for rare occasions sat.

"I do not—" I started, trying to think of the last time I'd brought someone home with me.

Not that my happiness relied on it, but it was nice to let loose sometimes.

"Fine," I conceded and grabbed the black heels.

"You're allowed to have a bit of fun on occasion," he reminded me.

"I know. I just feel like I can't stop to breathe until I make it out of here," I admitted.

"You know, it's not so bad here," he said.

Ah, the conversation I avoided. The one I knew came with a world of hurt at the reality that someday, I would have to leave him.

"I know, and you know I love the people here."

"But it's not enough?" he asked.

"I have to see what else is out there, before I chicken out and get stuck here with only regrets and empty dreams."

He nodded.

"Come with me," I told him. "New York is the hub of publishing. You'd be right at home there too."

"I wish I could," he said. "But that's your dream. I'm already living mine." He smiled gently and put a hand on my shoulder. I pulled him in to a hug and realized I was trembling again.

Fear of not knowing what would happen had sunk its claws into me. "I'm sorry," I whispered, my voice cracking.

"Never apologize for being true to yourself. I want

you to get everything you've dreamed of, and if that's New York, I will be the first one there, helping you unload your boxes when you move."

I pulled back to find his face completely serious. "I appreciate that," I said.

"Now let's get you to this party. I swear, if you're late to this, I will never forgive myself."

"I have all night, Felix," I said, knowing the lights on the estate never faded until the following morning every year.

"You're going to need it," he said and winked.

I rolled my eyes and finished my makeup, adding the finishing touch of silver eyeshadow.

"Fucking gorgeous," Felix complimented.

"You're required to say that," I noted.

"Maybe." He shrugged. "But right now, I mean it."

"Mhm," I answered, tossing lip gloss into the small black purse I settled on bringing.

Felix grabbed my arm and turned me toward him. "Sloane, seriously," he said. "I know I don't know everything that goes on at work, but whatever the fuck they said to have you so set on this, they are a bunch of dicks. If anyone can get this article written, it's you."

"Thanks," I whispered.

"Now go have fun while you do it," he said with a peck to my cheek.

I finished grabbing what I needed, and together, we made our way downstairs.

"Be safe," he said before walking me out.

"I will," I promised, stopping at the end of my walkway to give him a quick hug before turning in the direction of Hollow House.

CHAPTER 6

A CAR PICKED me up a block away from my house and drove me to the outskirts of town. It pulled up to the gate, which was the first time I had ever seen it open. The long, looping driveway was filled with other cars dropping off guests.

Men and women dressed to the nines stepped out and up the stone steps leading into the black brick mansion. My arms wrapped around my torso, self-conscious of my simple black dress as I stepped out of the car.

The second I shut the door, the driver took off. There was no going back now. I gripped the invitation tightly and climbed the same stairs as everyone else. No one was recognizable, masks covering most of their faces. Their outfits, however, told me they were not from town, wealthier individuals. No one in this town could afford the gems encrusting their bodies.

A man just outside the main door held out a hand to me, and I paused for a minute, confused whether he knew who I was. Was he offering me a hand to enter?

His eyes drifted down, and I realized I still held the invitation tightly in my palm. I held it out slowly to him, and he grabbed it from me. His gaze raked over it for a minute, and my breath caught in my throat, wondering if this was a mistake. Was the entire thing a hoax? That simple piece of paper couldn't really be my ticket in…

He stepped aside and silently ushered me through the door.

I moved before I could back out.

I stepped inside, immediately greeted by a woman holding a tray of drinks. The goblets had black metal stems, designed to look like a skeleton hand. I smiled, the design a silly little piece of Halloween décor—definitely not as horrifying as I expected.

"Welcome to Hollow House," the woman said, her voice sweet and soothing.

Her voice was only slightly muffled by the mask she wore. It covered the lower half of her face, black material with a silver design.

I could just barely see the room beyond her. The hall opened into a large space filled with voices.

"Um, hi. Where should I go?" I asked, a bit over-whelmed.

"Welcome to Hollow House," she repeated in the same muffled voice.

The woman handed me one of the drinks, and I politely accepted before moving on, trying not to over-think the entire interaction. The liquid burned as it passed my lips, and I took a large sip, needing the courage.

I pushed onward, following the others. Each stopped at the entrance to a small room to the side, and I realized it was a coat check. I hadn't worn one and went to turn away, but a huge mass stopped me, hands on my shoulders spinning me back around.

"That needs to stay," he ordered.

I followed his gaze down to my purse. "It's just my purse," I answered.

"It's the rules," he answered firmly. His arms crossed over his chest, letting go of me and letting me decide. "If you want to stay, it needs to remain here for tonight."

I glanced back at the door, wondering if I should just take this out. It would be easy enough to leave and call a car home. This was my last chance.

But I'd only just begun. I would never escape the small town life if I didn't take this chance.

I took the bag off my shoulder and passed it over to

a petite woman wearing the same mask as the woman at the door. She took the bag and disappeared. When she came back, she nodded to the next attendee.

"No ticket?" I asked, confused.

She shook her head and continued to reach around me to the next person. How would I grab my items later? I was pushed to the back by others filing in after. I tried to regain my focus and spun to follow others into the party. They moved quickly, and many passed by me, my feet moving far slower.

A couple already enjoyed themselves, making out against the wall of the hallway. The woman's moan met my ears, and I tried to keep my eyes forward as I passed. I wasn't used to such open displays of affection. Every rumor that floated around about this event all agreed on one detail: Hollow House was a pleasure house, one that held your deepest desires and encouraged you to let go.

I couldn't blame them for doing just that.

Maybe that was what I needed to do. Let go a little. Get laid.

Certainly the second one.

The moment I stepped foot into the main room, I felt watched. The chilling feeling washed over me, even in the sea of people. Where did they all come from if not from town? There wasn't a single person I'd met who had been fortunate enough to be invited.

Performers were placed on slight platforms throughout the room. Some did routines with poles. I watched in awe, completely impressed by their strength and flexibility. I went to pull out my phone but realized it was in the purse they confiscated.

I would have to remember all my notes for the article without writing them down.

No problem. I could still do this.

I watched mesmerized as women in tiny gold body-suits danced around the poles, walking on air and spinning around them. Their core strength held them up, and I could barely tear my eyes away.

"Appetizer?" a man in the same mask as the other workers asked.

Their clothing all differed, other than the black color scheme, but the masks were unmistakably the same. I guessed that was how they differentiated themselves from attendees. Each attendee wore a mask covering their eyes, whereas these masks covered their mouths. It muffled their voices, but I still managed to hear the question.

"Thank you," I said, grabbing a small skewer off the platter.

The food was divine, and I licked the sauce off my lips as I finished the last bite. Before I could even search for a trash, a waiter appeared to grab it. They came out of nowhere and disappeared before I could even question it. I spotted a few here and there throughout the crowd, but otherwise, they were completely ghosts.

There weren't signs to direct attendees toward other portions of the house, but I watched a few couples slip from the room, assuming the true party happened behind closed doors.

Further into the room, I spotted a DJ in a similar mask to the workers standing behind a table and playing the music that blasted through the room. The space was dimly lit, with only colored lights along the walls providing the majority of the light, color changing with the music.

A body knocked into me, and I was brushed to the side. People carried on without noticing me, and the overwhelming feeling that I didn't belong slammed into me. Some people chatted in corners, catching up, the masks not a barrier. I had no idea who anyone was, and the masks made it impossible to recognize anyone. I knew it was for privacy, especially in a place with such a reputation, but it was irking me.

I took the last sip of the drink in my hands, glancing around for one of the waiters to hand the glass off to. Instead, I found a table in the corner, where I spotted a few more abandoned glasses waiting to be taken.

I walked over and plopped the skeleton hand glass down. Then, I glanced around the room, trying to calculate where to head next. If I wanted to write a comprehensive article, one that would shock and delight people, I needed to see everything this place had to offer. All of it, the more shocking the better, needed to be covered.

My eyes landed on a man standing across the room. The only reason I spotted him was because the chair he sat in was raised above the crowd, on a dais of sorts.

I almost laughed, the chair resembling a throne. Who the fuck did this guy think he was? Royalty?

The picture was comical. This was a house of pleasures, a mansion filled with sins and desires that could make even the most adventurous blush…

A touch to my shoulder startled me, and I nearly jumped out of my skin. Why was I still so on edge, even inside, seeing how normal the party actually was?

I turned to find a man a few inches taller watching me. His Armani suit told me he was wealthy, certainly not a local.

"You're new here," he observed.

"I am," I confirmed, not seeing a reason to lie. Many attendees were probably annual invites. It made sense since no one from town was ever invited. The guest list appeared extremely curated. If only I could find out exactly who was on that list…

"Would you like a tour of the offerings?" he asked, a dark look in his gaze.

I recoiled from his outstretched hand. I hated the way the question sounded. Felix encouraged me to let loose, to possibly hook up with someone, but this didn't seem to be an opportunity I was eager to take.

"No, thank you," I declined.

He cocked his head, looking me over like I was a mystery to him. "Want another drink?" the man asked.

"No, I am all set," I assured him.

I needed a different excuse, because the typical polite yet uninterested tone was not working. This guy was persistent.

And not in an asshole type of way. It was more in a way that he wasn't used to having anyone uninterested in him. His face contorted, trying to make sense of the words coming from my mouth all while trying new ways to ask for my attention.

A presence behind me caught his attention, and as it closed in on us, my entire body tensed. The familiar feeling of being watched returned. I didn't get a chance for my body to catch up to my mind before my unwanted company opened his mouth.

"She's yours?"

A look of both horror and surprise flashed across his face, and my heart stopped.

CHAPTER 7

SHE WAS MINE.

The second I laid eyes on her, in that tiny little black dress that hugged her hips, I knew I needed a bite. I needed to bend her over a table and take her right there.

The way she walked through the crowd, lost, looking for someone to step in and guide her—it was all the invitation I needed.

I stood from the chair I lounged in, keeping watch. One night a year, I allowed the patrons of Hollow House to give in to their deepest desires. It kept them thankful throughout the year. Obedient. Loyal to one single person: the shadow who watched over them, guided them, provided them a sanctuary from the world that denied us.

She would be next.

I took a step down from the dais the chair sat on, watching her brown hair disappear into the crowd. I'd hunt her down and find out exactly what she desired.

The thought of my cock inside her, stretching her, pushed me down the next step.

She would join us.

Before the night was over, I would make her mine.

CHAPTER 8

"There you are, love," a deep voice whispered in my ear, their breath tickling my neck.

My core warmed at the way the word sounded on his lips, and I turned to find the man I spotted earlier behind me. Tattoos covered his body, his dark hair swept perfectly out of place.

His dark suit matched my dress, and I let out a slight sigh of relief that I hadn't messed up the attire to the extent I thought. His own mask was black, with similar gold detailing to the patterns on my own. Was that on purpose?

"If you'll excuse us," he said, nodding to the man who had been vying for my attention.

The other man respectfully backed away and left without another word.

"Do I know you?" I asked, his presence almost familiar.

"Not in the sense you ask," he answered, taking a step closer. His muscular frame pressed against me, and I tilted my head in confusion.

"Who are you?" I asked, genuine curiosity taking over.

It was for the article, I told myself. Everything I did tonight was for the sake of my work. I needed to put in every last effort I could to find a story here, one beyond this being a night club-esque sex party. There were far more rooms to explore in the house, and if this man could lead me to them, I welcomed it.

"There are no names here," he answered, avoiding the question. Everyone around us wore similar masks, their faces shrouded behind them.

"Well, what can I call you then?" I asked, crossing my arms.

If he wouldn't say who he was, that was fine. I was used to doing a little digging for the information I wanted. Never once did I think building this story would be easy.

"Many here refer to me as the Wraith. It's not a name I gave myself, but you're welcome to use it if you insist on something."

I let out a soft laugh at the absurdity of the nickname. Did people actually call him that?

46

It felt silly to me, but I went along with it anyway. Perhaps it was part of the allure of the night—one night to live your deepest desires and be whoever you wanted. A familiar concept on Halloween, not so far from reality that I couldn't play along.

"Okay, *Wraith*," I started. "Tell me, why was I invited here?"

He reached out and grabbed my waist, pulling me harder against him, which I didn't think was possible. I could feel his entire body pressed into me, parts hardening in my presence…

Nope, I shoved the thought from my mind as quickly as I could.

"Tell me, Sloane: why did you answer the call?" he asked.

The question and use of my name caught me off guard. I tried to cover it with a smile and nervous laugh, but he still watched me with the same intensity, seeing right through it. I tried to think of an excuse, but something told me he would see through that too.

Instead, I went with the truth.

"I'm writing an article on Hollow House," I stated, watching his face for a hint of anything to give me answers. He remained unmoved. "Which I suppose you already knew, if you know who I am," I guessed.

That made him grin. "No one comes here without

my permission. I've created a haven away from the world, one prying eyes need not see."

"Then why allow me here? Why invite me?"

"Because I know you'll never publish that article," he stated, not an ounce of doubt in his voice.

I scoffed. This article was my ticket out, the break I needed. Absolutely nothing was keeping me from that —not shitty bosses, not catty women at work, and certainly not this masked man. "And what makes you say that?"

It was his turn to laugh.

"I know people," he answered, dipping his head down to my ear. "And I know you better than you think," he whispered.

"Oh, really?" I challenged. "You know me so well?"

He ginned at my challenge, and my core warmed at the intensity of his gaze. It was almost uncomfortable, but I found I couldn't look away.

"I know you've been observing this entire room since you got here," he said.

I scoffed. "I am a journalist," I said, almost disappointed he'd said the most obvious thing.

"I wasn't finished, my love," he tsked.

There was that word again. *Love.* I hated that I loved the way it sounded when it rolled off his tongue

—a tongue I imagined doing depraved things to my body as I watched him lick his lips almost hungrily.

"You've watched this room without joining in, but I can tell you wish to. So tell me, love: what is your darkest desire?" he asked.

My mouth opened, but words failed to come out. I wanted to tell him he was wrong, that I was solely here for the article, but then I remembered Felix's words. Even my best friend thought I needed to get laid.

He leaned forward, his mouth grazing my ear. "You can have anyone here," he whispered in my ear. "Who will it be, love?"

I glanced past him, barely able to look around his large, muscular frame. "Him?" I asked and nodded to a man watching us, sipping from a glass of wine.

"Of course," he assured me and dipped his head in, nipping at my skin and sending shivers down my spine.

Instinctively, I moved my head to bare my neck to him, a complete stranger. I needed to get a grip, but I couldn't. He'd roped me into his game, and admittedly, I was having fun.

"And her?" I gasped as his hand rubbed down my back.

He glanced to the side, following my gaze to a woman pretending to be uninterested, but I'd caught her many sideways gazes.

"Is that what you want?" he asked. "Perhaps both of them at once?"

I shuddered at the thought of the man taking me while I devoured the beautiful woman.

"Maybe," was all I could force out as he pushed up against me. I could feel how hard he was behind the black slacks he wore.

"You can have whoever, but just remember, at the end of the night, you're still mine."

Mine.

The last word came out on a possessive growl. My core heated, and I knew if he slipped his hand under my dress, he'd find just how much his words turned me on.

His hand slid down the front of me and to the top of my thigh.

"Not here," I said, sucking in a gasp.

I tried to push away from him, to turn around and see who else had their eyes on us, but his strong hand wrapped possessively around me and pulled me back. Pressed against him, I felt his cock hard against my ass.

"Do not move," he ordered.

The low command made my center slick. Without even touching me beneath my dress, this man already had me wet and ready.

"We have rules I need to go over before I allow you

to play in my home," he said in a low tone. "The first is that desires and pleasure are a priority here. We do not judge what others partake in so long as it does not cross any boundaries."

I sucked in a breath, his lips pressing against my neck.

"The second is that if you do not want something, all you need to do is say so. Everyone abides by the same safety word. Just say *pumpkin*, and they'll stop."

I almost laughed at the absurdity of the word, but I supposed that was why it was picked.

"And if I don't want them to stop?" I dared to ask, afraid if I said nothing, he would leave.

"You'll find out, love," he whispered, and his hand slipped lower down my thigh.

My cheeks reddened, embarrassment grabbing hold of me as I realized I was still in the room full of people.

"You can't seriously—" I started, the words coming out almost jumbled.

His hand stopped me before I could finish. His fingers bunched the fabric of my dress, pulling at it.

No one around us seemed to care. I didn't know whether I hoped it stayed that way or not. The idea of all these people watching us, seeing how much I wanted him, made my chest ache with both fear and desire.

His fingers found the hem of my dress and brushed against my bare thigh. I tried to turn into him, but his other hand stopped me, holding me in place.

"Wraith," I moaned, his fingers dancing over my skin.

His hand slipped under my dress, hovering over the thin lace panties I wore. The second I felt him tug the material, I knew I was exposed to the room. What was I doing?

"We can't do this here!" I insisted, a bit of urgency creeping into my voice.

His fingers brushed against my slick folds, and I moaned, unable to get more words out. My back arched against him, and he continued to tease my entrance, his fingers feeling how wet I was already.

He tipped my head up with his other hand and kissed me. His hand held my chin, wrapping around my neck. The slight pressure there heightened what I felt between my legs.

"You don't truly believe that," he said.

A few pairs of wandering eyes found us, watching as I remained helplessly pinned to the Wraith, my pussy exposed to the room as he teased against my entrance.

My cheeks heated an impossibly deep shade of red. "We have an audience," I choked out.

"Let them watch," he said, his voice stern and dripping with desire.

A single finger pushed into me, and the moan I let out was loud enough to draw more attention. People whispered and watched as he continued to thrust in and out of me. I craved more. A single finger wasn't enough.

The feeling kept my focus solely on him and not the attention we'd gathered.

"More," I whimpered as he pushed his finger in and out, the palm of his hand rubbing against my clit, the other fingers grazing and teasing me.

"Anything you desire, love," he whispered, and I tensed as two more fingers slid in.

Pain was the first thing I felt, my entire body tensing at the shocking pressure and amount filling me. I had asked for this, craved it, but my body wasn't used to it. There hadn't been many men or women I'd seen lately.

I bit my lip, trying to hide my cry of both pain and pleasure. The metallic taste of blood was enough to snap my eyes open, surprise waking me from my pleasure-filled state. I spotted all the people watching us. Some had turned away, occupied with their own explorations of pleasure. Others watched, the intensity of their gaze enough to make me falter.

"Enough of them," the Wraith said sternly and flipped me around to face him.

He kissed my lips, and I closed my eyes, trying to

fully accept all the pleasures he offered. His kiss was gentle at first, easing me into it all, but it turned desperate as we went. He pulled out the three fingers to give me a second of relief before readjusting his approach.

He moved himself behind me, guiding me to the table nearby. His strong hands bent me over the table and pulled my hair back, holding it in a tight grip. The slight pain at his tug had me gasping.

This time, when he slipped his fingers back inside me, only two pushed into my pussy. The third moved to a new spot, one I had never explored with anyone else.

I moaned against his lips as the finger entered my ass and pushed in rhythm with the other too. I became entirely overwhelmed by the sensation. Nothing in my mind made sense, and my vision turned to a complete blur.

"Fuck," I gasped.

"You like that, don't you, love?" the Wraith asked.

At this point, I was convinced every last set of eyes in the room had to be on us, but I was too distracted to look. To be honest, I didn't care anymore. Whatever this was, whatever the Wraith wanted to give to me, I wanted it.

I wanted all of it.

I just hadn't known it until that second.

"More," I begged.

I heard the low chuckle that came from him before he pushed into me harder and faster. All my senses went into overdrive. I could barely feel the rest of my body, numb with pleasure.

"That's it, love. Come for me," he demanded as my pussy clenched around him.

My thighs trembled, and his hand holding my hair tugged lightly, encouraging me. I let out a loud moan as I toppled over the edge, my orgasm slamming into me. The Wraith knew it too, still fingering me through the pleasure. My entire body shook, my head dizzy as he pulled his fingers out and helped me stand to adjust my dress. By the time I turned to face him, the attendees picked up again, ignoring us completely.

Had I imagined them watching in the first place?

There was no possible way they didn't see us.

"That was—" I stopped; no words could properly describe it. "Thanks," I managed instead.

"No need to thank me, love," he answered. "We are just getting started."

That felt like both a threat and a promise. My toes curled in response, my cheeks still red with desire.

"I'm going to grab you a drink," the Wraith offered, and before I could accept, he wandered into the crowd.

The feeling of heat throughout my body became overwhelming. Usually, after an orgasm, it subsided quickly, but not now. No, I was far too aware of how dizzy I felt, the sweat beading on my forehead. The bodies packed into the room didn't help, contributing to how hot it was.

My vision danced with little black dots, and I knew I had to move quickly.

CHAPTER 9

I needed air.

The heat of my orgasm coursed through my body. My cheeks reddened, and I remained frozen long after the Wraith slipped away into the crowd. A waitress passed by with a tray of drinks in the little skull hand glasses, and I snatched one. I drank it quickly, the faint taste of wine washing down the back of my throat. It did little to settle the heat inside me.

Nearby, I spotted a sliding door leading out back, and I pushed through the crowd toward it. Sweaty bodies pressed against me, swaying and dancing to the music.

A body pressed up against my back, the muscular figure so close, I could sense their breathing. Had he come back for me?

Strong arms wrapped around my waist, and the

figure bent down to whisper in my ear over the sound of the music. "Do you have a desire you'd like fulfilled?"

I didn't recognize the voice. It was higher and different from the Wraith's.

I turned to find a different handsome man staring down at me. He was the type I usually went after the few times I allowed myself a break.

"I'm just heading outside," I said politely.

"Would you like me to join?" he asked with a questioning glance.

The question seemed good-natured, but for some reason, everything inside me screamed no. I still couldn't get the other man out of my head.

Maybe Felix was right. Maybe I did need to get laid if a single orgasm had me this focused on a random man I just met.

Beyond the man, I caught sight of movement in the crowd. The familiar dark eyes caught mine, and I blinked a few times, wondering if I imagined them. A second later, the Wraith was gone. Maybe it was just a trick of my mind, or maybe the wine was going straight to my head.

Shit.

The guy still stared at me, now like I head two heads.

"Sorry, I'm okay. I just need some air. Too much wine," I said with a weak smile.

I slipped away before he could say anything else.

Crisp autumn air slammed into me the second I stepped outside. An extensive garden greeted me, and I followed a small stone path into it.

This far into the season, many plants from summer had died off, but some clung to life still. Leaves crunched beneath my black heels, littering the ground around me.

The Wraith had not followed.

Had part of me hoped he would?

This was a house of pleasures, I reminded myself. He was here for that. He teased me and took pleasure from me, and now, he'd moved on.

My skin crawled with the feeling of eyes on me, even outside alone. I couldn't shake the feeling I was always being watched.

I stopped in front of a group of dahlias, their orange and red colors deeply vibrant.

Instinct forced me to lift my gaze, and a shadow movement caught my eye. I tried to follow it but lost it in the darkness.

My heart raced, picking up in speed each second the silence remained, but I couldn't find what had caused the shadow.

I stared across the landscape, narrowing my focus.

Nothing else around me mattered. I felt like my sanity was slowly slipping.

Bang. Bang. Bang.

I jumped, startled by the sudden loud sound.

A pounding behind me sent a shiver down my spine. I turned, my heart racing, not initially finding anything. My gaze swept across the garden, and the pounding continued. I lifted my stare to the mansion, and movement in one of the windows on the second floor caught my eye.

My feet instinctively moved forward. The closer I got, I could make out the silhouette of a woman. The pounding grew more furious.

I stopped when I finally had a good view, and my jaw dropped. The woman in the window waved frantically to me. She glanced over her shoulder and pounded again at the window. I stood frozen with fear, watching in horror.

Where was she?

I had to get to her, to help her. Was she hurt?

A shadow crept over her, and the look of terror that spread across her face kept me paralyzed. All I could do was helplessly watch.

She mouthed something, and I swore it looked like *help*.

A hand wrapped around her and covered her mouth. One moment, she was there, and the next, she was ripped backward. I couldn't see who grabbed her, but the second she disappeared, I moved.

I sprinted back inside, straight into the group of people still dancing to the music. I pushed through bodies grinding on each other, enjoying their pleasures on the dance floor.

"Help," I said meekly.

No one paid me any attention.

"Help," I said a bit more forcefully, drawing some attention, but no one moved.

I sprinted through the crowd and found the staircase I'd seen when I entered the house. My feet hurried, taking them two at a time. Fuck, why did it feel like I was moving in slow motion? Every second passed was one wasted.

Upstairs was more of a maze than the garden or first floor. Which window was it? A few down in the left of the house maybe?

I walked down the hallway and started trying doors I knew had windows facing the back of the house. The first door I tried led to an empty room. A single bed sat inside, alongside minimal furniture, but not the woman.

I tried the next one, the door locked. Fuck, I hadn't thought about what to do if the door was locked. Was she inside? Could she hear me trying to get to her?

I pounded on the locked door, hoping someone

inside would open. If she was in there, perhaps my noise and persistence could stop whatever was happening. I pulled back my arm again to hit the door, but it stopped. A strong hand caught my wrist and pulled me back. My body spun, slamming into a massive wall.

Not a wall—a man. The man from before stared down at me, still holding my wrist. He cocked his head, his eyes questioning me.

"What's wrong?" he asked.

"That woman!" I said, trying to catch my breath. "She needs help."

His brows furrowed only slight.

"What woman?" he asked.

"I saw her," I said, trying to calm myself down and reasonably explain what I'd seen.

He didn't ask anything further, instead moving me back from the door. I opened my mouth to protest until I watched him knock on the door.

"Open," he demanded in a stern, powerful tone.

I watched, speechless, as the door cracked open, and the second the man behind it saw the Wraith, he opened it further.

"Apologies," the Wraith started. "My love believes she saw someone calling out for help from outside."

The way he said it out loud made me realize how insane I sounded, but there was also almost a threatening piece to it. He wrapped a hand around my waist, pulling me closer to his body.

"That was my fault," a woman said confidently, stepping forward into view. "Got a little too into the role, I'm afraid."

Her bright doe-like eyes stared at me with sincerity. The man on the other hand looked pissed at me for being a cock block.

"Sorry," I said quietly, feeling foolish.

"Don't apologize," the Wraith said without elaboration.

I looked up to find him staring with gentle composure, almost sympathetic. The other man made a sound that resembled a scoff, and the Wraith glared at him, forcing him to back down.

These people listened to him, respected him.

I already suspected he was the one in charge. Perhaps he owned the entire estate, but this was all the confirmation I needed.

"We will leave you now," the Wraith said and backed away, grabbing my hand and pulling me from my state of shock.

I followed wordlessly down the hall, trying not to let my embarrassment show. I'd disrupted their night, the single reason people came to Hollow House, to fulfill their desires. The thought stopped me in my tracks. My feet refused to move further, and my grip broke from the Wraith's.

The Wraith stalked back toward me. With each step, I wanted to shrink further into myself. I was a nobody. Why was he so set on me?

"Come back to me, love," he said and held out a hand.

"I should go," I said but didn't move. "This was a mistake—"

"Was it?" he asked. "If this was truly a mistake, I'll walk you to the gate myself."

I wanted to move, to go home to my little house and curl up in my bed the rest of the night, but my feet betrayed me. I screamed at myself to move, and still, nothing.

His gaze had me pinned. "Tell me what you want, love," he ordered.

To leave.

To write my article.

To run and never look back.

"You."

CHAPTER 10

MY LIPS SLAMMED INTO HIS, his strong arms pushing me back against the wall. My back hit it with a tiny thud, but I didn't care. I was far too consumed by him.

His tongue slipped past my lips, begging me to give him more.

The cold wall against my back was the only thing keeping the burning desire under my skin somewhat in check.

Wetness pooled at my center, and his hands slipped down my body. Before I could stop him, embarrassed by the effect he so easily had on me, he slipped a hand under my dress and tugged at the lace thong. Two fingers slipped under the fabric, and he pulled back from my mouth.

"Is all of this for me, love?" he drawled. His dark eyes clung to mine, and my entire body caught aflame.

If a stranger could turn me on so quickly, I was far more desperate than I thought.

I nodded, unable to form a coherent sentence. The Wraith brought the two fingers to his mouth and sucked them clean, his tongue lapping up every last bit of me.

His other arm held my waist, thankfully, or I would've collapsed into a puddle watching him.

"More," I groaned, the word slipping from my mouth.

"Say that again, and I'll give you anything you desire," he warned.

"More," I whimpered.

The Wraith dropped to his knees before me, his hand lifting my dress and settling on my waist. One moved just to lift my leg and place it over his shoulder.

Before I could figure out what he was doing, his hand tugged at my thong, the fabric tearing with a sting to my flesh.

A gasp slipped form my lips, which morphed into a moan the second his tongue flicked against my slit. It explored every inch of my center as his hands held my waist, keeping me firmly where he wanted. My hands slipped into his messy brown hair. Steps echoed just down the hall from us, but I didn't care.

I tried to bend my knees a little, my pussy begging for more. One of his hands slipped to my inner thigh, rubbing lazy circles against my clit, his tongue slipping inside me.

I moaned, unable to hide any of the pleasure he pulled from me. If this was the way Hollow House could fill my deepest desires, I'd gladly stay like this all night.

The article slipped away slowly, and I let my mind wander to thought of the Wraith and the pleasure he could make me feel.

His tongue worked faster as I whimpered, realizing I was so close to tumbling off that edge.

His tongue pulled out from me at the last moment, and before I could express my displeasure, two fingers slipped inside me. They curled, and my entire body shuddered. Another two pumps and I lost control. A cry of pleasure rang out as my orgasm slammed into me. My entire body shook as he continued to work me through it, my vision going blurry and my knees buckling.

The Wraith slowly lowered me to the floor, my back to the wall. He watched me, his dark gaze taking in every last detail.

As he kneeled in front of me, I could see his face clearly now. The way his dark stubble covered his chin completely. The tattoos that snaked up his neck and dipped beneath the collar of his shirt. I wanted to reach out and cup his face, but the pure heat in his gaze kept me pinned to the wall instead. I couldn't move.

Instead, I opened my mouth and was shocked by what came out.

"What did she mean?" I asked.

"Who, love?" he asked, tipping his head slightly.

"That woman," I muttered. "What did she mean *the role*?"

An amused smile grew on his lips, and he reached out to brush a pink strand of hair out of my face. My heart pounded, waiting for him to answer. His grip tightened on the back of my neck and pulled me in closer, the possessive touch warming my core again.

"Fear," he whispered.

"Fear?"

He nodded, and my hands found his knee to steady myself. The pleasure of the previous few minutes had completely subsided, and my breathing returned to normal, rather than the ragged breaths I couldn't contain after what he'd done.

"Fear. The way adrenaline rushes through your body when you're terrified…it changes something in you. For some, it is pleasurable, a high they chase," he explained.

"I don't understand…"

My mind couldn't wrap itself around doing such a thing. How could being terrified be enjoyable? I hated the way my heart raced and sat in my throat when I was afraid. I hated the lack of control I had over my body.

Before I could express any of that to him or ask a question, he gripped my face firmly in his hands and gave me a single order.

"Run, and you'll find out, love."

CHAPTER II

At first, I didn't move, unsure if I heard him correctly. Did he mean it? Where was I supposed go?

"Run, love," he whispered into my ear.

Without thinking, I took off. My pace was slow, my heels preventing me from fully running, but I tried my best.

The halls were confusing, and each turn I committed to had me further lost. I couldn't turn back, not when he'd ordered me to run.

Something about the way he spoke, the command so confident—I couldn't ignore it.

I slowed down to look back over my shoulder. The Wraith rounded the corner, and I smiled playfully, but then my heart nearly stopped. The glint of metal in his hands was so small, I thought I missed it. There was no possible way I was correct.

But the longer I stood without moving as he gained on me, the more unmistakable the object became.

In his hands, he twirled and toyed with a knife.

My heart stopped all together, and I choked on a gasp.

Move, I commanded myself.

Fucking move!

I ran faster down the hall, away from the man I was now convinced was trying to murder me. Was this because of my small freak out before?

Is this what took place in this house?

Why no one knew the secrets and inner workings of Hollow House?

The mansion was a labyrinth, endless halls and turns that looped in circles. I kept trying to get away, only to find myself closer and closer to the predator stalking me.

Out of breath, I turned down one last hall with a couple of doors lining it. At the end, a staircase led downstairs. I prayed he would assume I had chosen the stairs. Before he could turn the corner and catch up, I slipped quietly inside the third door. Even if he checked the first room, would he waste time checking the rest?

Inside was a bed that looked unused for years, a small nightstand, and deep maroon curtains covering the single window. To my right, a closet called my attention, and I ran for it. Slipping inside, I closed the door as softly as I could, terrified any tiny noise would give me away.

Was this his whole plan? Get my attention and have me drop my walls so he could kill me? Was this why no one knew what went on inside Hollow House? People didn't survive long enough to share?

Eventually, I heard the footsteps echoing in the hall, slow and meticulous. I held my breath, waiting for them to move on. Items brushed against the back of my neck, sending shivers down my spine, and I squeezed my eyes shut.

The footsteps stopped, and I thought he moved on. I could wait a few more minutes then slip out and run for the gate. If I could at least make it down to the main party, the cover of the crowd and so many witnesses had to be a way to stop his chase.

A creaking noise pulled me from the thought, and I held my breath, terrified it would give me away.

"Did you think you could hide here forever?" he asked just before he tore open the closet door.

"No, please!" I screamed, pulling my arm away, but failing.

He dragged me over to the bed and pushed me onto it. My back slammed into it, and the Wraith from earlier, the man who gracefully wrung pleasure from me, was gone, replaced by a predator who didn't give a shit about being gentle.

He pinned me to the bed, my arms above my head. I writhed beneath him, but he didn't budge.

"Please," I whispered. "Don't hurt me. I won't write the article."

It was the only thing I could think to say. It wouldn't matter if I was dead. If he killed me, the information I gathered here would remain safe forever. Why was I even bothering? I thought of work and Felix, my family. Would anyone notice I was gone? Would they come looking?

I suspected Hollow House had a way to deal with that too.

The Wraith climbed over me, using his weight to keep me in place. He let go of my wrists, and I clawed at him. My entire body thrashed, but the harder I fought, the more his devilish grin spread.

His hands spread my legs, and pulled my dress up revealing my bare pussy to him, the thong already destroyed earlier in the night by him.

He dipped the knife closer to my leg, and I stilled, afraid any sudden movement would cause him to cut me.

"Don't move," he ordered.

For some reason, I listened. His tone didn't promise the death I'd become so sure he intended to deliver. Instead, it dripped with desire and lust.

The knife grazed lightly against my leg, but the tip

was sharp enough to cut. It was quick and small, not enough to seriously hurt me. I felt a sting in between my thighs and instinctively wanted to reach down, but he stopped my moving hand.

I felt blood drip down my leg, panic taking over. I tried to move from under him, but his weight held me in place again. All I could do was lift my head to see the small beads of blood on the tip of his knife before he placed it to the side..

"Please," I whimpered.

"Like the rest of us," he said, admiring his work, "you bleed."

His fingers trailed up my thigh, rubbing blood along my leg. I could feel the sticky drips now smeared against my leg.

"That's what connects us all," he stated. "Everyone here bleeds the same. No matter how badly society wanted to toss us aside, we are all the same underneath."

The words made zero sense, and I tensed as his fingers moved higher. He found my center and ran a finger along it, wet beyond my control. My body still reacted to his touch, regardless of how afraid I was of him. He dipped a finger inside me, and I let out an involuntary moan.

"Such a good fucking girl."

Once. Twice. Three times, he pushed into me before pulling his fingers out again.

He ran them down my leg in the same path he'd followed before. He lifted them to his lips, and I could see the mix of my blood and slickness as he licked his fingers clean.

My stomach tensed in a mix of desire and fear.

The Wraith picked the knife up again, and I squirmed under him, afraid of how far he would go next. My legs slammed shut, and that earned me a deadly glare.

"Do not ever close this from me, love," he warned. He pushed them apart again easily, and I barely fought against him.

My mind screamed at me to run, to put an end to this all, but my body craved his touch. He hadn't hurt me. I wanted to push that limit, see how far he would take it, feel the pleasure he promised me.

"Stop," I tried, unsure if I meant it for him or myself.

"Stop what, love?" he asked, pushing a finger back inside me.

He curled it, and I arched my back, wanting more of that feeling and pressure. He refused to touch my clit, instead continuing with teasing pushes in and out of my pussy.

I let out a huff of frustration.

"Stop this?" he asked as he pushed a second finger inside me.

"No," I said without thinking.

"No?" he questioned and shifted to keep going. His fingers slid in and out in a rhythm I came to crave. The anticipation and absolute pleasure I felt were enough to make my head spin.

Maybe that was why I made the decision. It could be why I was allowing this insanity to continue. Or perhaps, I was just truly as twisted as him.

I shuddered both at the thought and the way his finger curled and stroked inside me.

Why did my entire core tense watching him take me in such a primal way?

"Wraith," I pleaded and warned all at once.

My own words were confused, partly begging him to keep going and partially terrified of what would happen if he did. He placed the knife to the side and climbed further over me.

"I'm going to teach you what happens to those who run from me," he growled.

His head dipped and kissed at my neck as I tilted my chin away. Strong hands positioned themselves next to my head, and I felt caged in, like an animal backed into a corner.

He told me to run. I was only following his orders...

I tensed as the nip of pain coursed over my skin, his teeth sinking into my neck. It was hard enough that I knew there'd be a bruise to remind me tomorrow morning. I was shocked it didn't draw blood.

He pulled back and picked up the knife from beside me. I moved to pull myself away, but his other hand grabbed my thigh and kept me in place.

"I want you to take this like a good girl," he ordered.

My eyes widened, seeing the hilt of the knife held up for me to see. He inched it closer to my center, and my entire body tensed in anticipation. Panic and fear coursed through me, but something else was there as well.

I wanted this, I realized. I wanted him inside me again.

As twisted and fucked up as it was, I wanted to feel what it was like to have the Wraith press his knife into me, to come on his weapon and watch the look of pure heat that crept into his gaze as I did.

I spread my legs and tried to will my body to relax.

The second the knife pressed to my entrance, I knew I was right. That last feeling was desire. My adrenaline spiked enough for my body to relax and allow the Wraith to slip the knife hilt inside me.

At first, it hurt. The object rubbed against me, raw and hard. The Wraith moved his finger against my clit, helping me ease the tension and urging my body to create the familiar wetness to help ease the pumping of the handle.

It was longer than most, and he held the knife at the closest point to the sharp blade. One wrong move from either of us, and one of us could end up seriously injured.

Why did that thought have my core warming? How sick and twisted was I?

"I need more," I begged, the feeling of the knife in me not enough.

"What do you desire, love?" he asked.

I was completely and utterly gone from who I was. There was no turning back after this. Whoever I was after would be a new person from whom I was stepping in to Hollow House.

"Ruin me," I demanded.

"Anything you desire, love," he said and pulled the knife out, tossing it to the side and helping me out of my dress.

He quickly unzipped his pants, and as he did, I unbuttoned most of his shirt. He finished the last two for me, exposing his beautiful body. It was covered in tattoos, ones I wanted to trace my fingers over.

Before I could get a good look at them, his cock thrust into me, and I let out a gasping moan.

At first, it hurt, his large cock stretching me in ways

I didn't think possible. I could feel every inch of him as he pushed fully into me.

"Finish me," I begged, wanting to feel the same pleasure he pulled from me twice already.

He continued to thrust into me over and over, my hand reaching down to find my clit to rub in lazy circles, intensifying the feeling. My pussy pulsed around each thrust of his cock.

"So fucking tight," he growled before pulling out and flipping me around.

I scrambled to get on my knees, my ass backing into him, knees spread for easier access.

I cursed as he pushed into me again, my entire body stumbling forward. I caught myself and arched my back, needing to feel him even better.

His hands gathered my long brown hair and pulled at it. The strands wrapped around his fists, and he tugged, the pain adding to the pleasure as I let out a deep moan.

His thrusts became more untamed, faster, and eventually, he let go of my hair to hold my hips. His hands pulled me back against him, and I could hear my ass slapping against him with each push and pull.

A deep, loud moan escaped my lips as I felt my body explode into tiny bursts of pleasure. He rode me through my orgasm, and my body almost went limp as he finished inside me. His cum leaked down my leg as he pulled out, and I felt the warmth of it running the same path as the cuts he made.

He turned me around, helping me lie on my back and regain my breath.

"This belongs to me," he said, running a finger along my folds. "You can have anything you desire here, but you answered my call." His dark eyes looked over my face for any hint of objection. "My desire is for you to be mine." After a second, he spoke again, before I could answer. "Who does this belong to?" he asked, and I know exactly what he wanted to hear.

Could I give him that?

"Love, don't test my patience," he warned, his hand hovering gently over my neck.

One forceful squeeze, and he'd cut off all my air. My back arched slightly, and I reached out to grab his wrist. Surprise flashed through his eyes, assuming I was about to defy him.

Instead, I tugged enough to move his hand firmly against my neck. The light pressure was enough to revive all the desire that had been coursing through me only minutes before.

"You," I answered quietly, my eyes heavy with exhaustion. "It all belongs to you."

CHAPTER 12

"Sloane?" a familiar voice gently called.

I was in the same room as before, rubbing sleep from my eyes.

I looked around, most of my surroundings a blur no matter what I did. I tried squinting and sitting up, but it was useless. The sheets were tucked up by my chin as I positioned myself to curl into the fetal position.

"Sloane," the voiced said again.

A figure moved, a mix of shadows and blur.

"Wraith?" I asked, my voice cracking and my throat dry.

I needed water or something to drink desperately. The figure moved closer, and I started to make out some of their features.

"Felix?" I questioned. "Why are you here?"

It didn't make sense, not unless it was something with the shop. Did they forget to drop off one of the orders for the party? But how did he find me? My head hurt and eyes burned.

"Sloane, are you alright? I had to check on you," he said.

"I'm fine," I answered, confused and exhausted.

I needed more sleep, not an interrogation. Why was he here? How was he here? My mind reached for answers and came up empty. The silky sheets of the bed felt cool against my skin, and their movement made me realize I still had no clothes on.

My hands instinctively pulled the sheets higher as my face heated.

"Why are you here?" I asked.

"It's complicated," he answered. "I just needed to know you were alright here."

I shook my head in confusion. The movement gave me the spins, my head pounding now. I wanted to give him an answer, but words wouldn't come. The more I tried, the more discomfort I felt. My hand flew to my throat, my esophagus stinging as I tried to force words out.

Felix backed away from the bed, watching me in horror. I grew more and more panicked, sitting up in the bed. I didn't care if my entire body was exposed; I felt like I was choking, unable to swallow or speak.

Air still flowed through my airway, and I tried to calm my breathing, but it was hard when panic and pain had grabbed hold of me. I heard a door open, and soon, strong arms wrapped around me.

"Sleep, love," he spoke. "It's only a dream."

The words were soothing, and I found myself finally able to take a deep breath. As I inhaled, I swore I could smell the familiar scent of the Wraith pressed against me.

Only a dream, I repeated in my mind. I couldn't speak, but I kept saying it over and over until I believed it. I nestled against him and let him stroke my hair. If this was a dream, I wasn't sure I ever wanted to wake up.

"It's time," a deep voice spoke from behind him, and the Wraith pulled back.

I wanted to scream, but still, no sound came out. A man stood in the doorway, his medical mask not the ones the attendees of Hollow House wore. My hands reached for the Wraith, but he slipped away, leaving me alone. My vision was still blurry, and I immediately lost sight of him.

The man moved forward, holding a large syringe.

I tried to fight it, but he held me down. As I kicked and thrashed, I realized there were multiple people holding me down. I looked to my left and spotted Felix, an apologetic look on his face. To my right, the Wraith gripped my arm, helping to pin me down.

I tried again to cry out, but only silence filled the air.

The needle jabbed into my thigh, and suddenly, I felt heavy. My eyes could barely stay open, and my body went limp. Everyone let go of me, backing away, watching me like I was a ticking time bomb.

Maybe I was.

I didn't fucking know anymore.

"Goodnight, love," the Wraith whispered, and it was the last thing I heard before the world went black.

CHAPTER 13

I woke from sleep when I heard a small beeping sound. I glanced around, noticing it was still pitch black outside. How long had I accidentally slept for?

Sitting up in a panic, I felt strong arms pull at my waist, trying to tug me back down. The unexpected touch startled me, and I jumped further away.

"Where am I?" I asked, wildly looking around. My mind felt blurry, and I grasped to remember what had happened before I passed out.

The Wraith sat up and grabbed my chin firmly, forcing me to look at him.

Right. Him.

"You're safe, love," he answered as he helped me lay back down next to him. The Wraith remained next to me, unmoving while my chest rose and fell at a fast pace. The adrenaline crash was intense, my body trembling.

"How long?" I asked, a bit embarrassed.

"Only an hour," he murmured, his fingers running along my cheek in reassurance.

The beeping sound started again, and I felt him reach to pull something from his pocket.

"Fuck," he muttered, pulling out a phone and opening it.

"Hmm?" I answered, fully turning toward him.

"I have something I have to handle."

I didn't expect more than a one night hook up, but after he declared me his for the rest of the night, I did expect more than this. A ridiculous excuse to slip away?

"I don't know you whatsoever. You could just tell me the truth and be done with me for the night," I said, a bit of a bite to my tone.

He moved so fast, I had no time to register as he climbed on top of me and pinned me to the bed. His weight shifted, his hard cock rubbing against my thigh.

"You feel that?" he asked. "That, love, is the effect you have on me. I would rather stay here and have you ride me until you see stars and scream my name, but I have a small matter to handle."

"I still don't know your name," I scoffed, unsure how much I believed him.

"You don't need to right now. All you need to know is you are mine, and you have learned nothing tonight if you think for a second I am done with you."

With that, he stood, grabbing his shirt from the end of the bed. He finished buttoning it on the way to the door.

"Don't wander too far," he said as he grabbed the handle. "I'll be back shortly."

He slipped out the door, shutting it quickly behind him. The click of it latching again had me sitting up and staring into the darkness. What the fuck was all of that?

My head was barely clear enough to think straight. The wine and sex had me all forms of fucked up. I need to wash up, splash some water on my face. I also needed to pee before I doomed myself to my worst nightmare: a UTI.

Not the parting gift I wanted to take home with me.

I far preferred to take with me a story that would be my ticket out of the town. I still didn't have the information I needed for any type of juicy article, but I was working on it. I was close, I could feel it. I just needed to stop getting distracted by sex.

The best sex I'd had in a long time, possibly ever. Okay, definitely ever.

But I wasn't about to tell him that. I sensed he

already had a big enough ego, and he didn't need more to fuel it.

I pulled myself out of the bed, refusing to sulk and wait for the mystery man to come back. He may have been great, fucking fantastic, but I also wasn't about to let myself become the woman who wasted the party waiting for him.

I at least needed to find a bathroom and clean up.

The hall was empty when I pulled the door open. I knew I was on the second floor, but I hadn't been paying attention when running for my life.

I walked for a while, hitting dead ends and trying to follow the sound of music I could faintly make out. Stairs appeared in front of me after far too long spent wandering the halls. They weren't the main staircase, but I imagined I could still get down to the party from them.

As I walked down, the music grew louder. It beckoned me back to the main room, begging me to join the festivities. I'd almost forgotten how many remained downstairs.

Eventually, I spotted a woman walking toward me and waved to her. She eyed me cautiously, and I realized how manic I looked, with my hair a tangled mess and my mask covering half my face.

Her own mask was a pastel pink, silver outlining the edges.

"Where is the bathroom?" I asked politely, needing to clean myself up.

"Right down that hall," the woman answered and hurried off before I could even thank her.

I noticed the narrow hall branching off to the right in front of me. It was not the same as any I'd gone down before.

A waitress appeared in the hall, carrying a tray of drinks and walking toward me. I could hear the music following from where she came as she offered me another drink of wine. I politely declined, my head feeling clouded.

Maybe it was the high of another orgasm, or perhaps I'd had too much to drink too fast.

I wandered down the hall, the instructions enough to get me away from the party. But once in the hall, I quickly realized how misguided I was.

Doors lined the walls, all unlabeled. I opened a few, closets and sitting rooms behind each. Nothing remotely close to a bathroom, though.

I turned down a hall that branched to the right, hopeful I'd find something. All this space—there had to be at least one around.

After many failed attempts, I finally found one in the furthest corner of the house. The door groaned as I pushed it open. The dim lights just barely lit the stalls enough to see. It wasn't quite what I was imagining in a mansion. Instead, it resembled more of a rundown school bathroom.

I picked the middle stall, realizing I had my pick with no attendees in the bathroom with me. The door shut behind me, and I had to fidget just to get the lock in place.

I peed as fast as I could, anxious to get back. The more time I spent away from the Wraith, the more I found my morals and plans going out the window.

My body craved his presence. The longer I was away from him, the more I itched to feel his touch again. I'd make my way back to the room he left me in and wait for him.

A small thud echoed through the bathroom, and I froze, standing up in the stall. Another guest had to have entered. I tried to catch a glimpse through the crack of the door, curious about each party goer. The more I learned, the more I could write for the article.

At first, I saw nothing. The longer I stared, I realized how ridiculous I was being. I smoothed out my dress, ready to step out and wash my hands. If someone was out there, I could see for myself then.

"Sloane."

The word was a whisper, barely even there. Did I even hear it?

The water dripped—perhaps it was that, the sound echoing and playing tricks on my mind.

I looked up through the crack, convinced I heard my name. I could just make out the sink and counter, water dripping and driving me crazy. The little sliver wasn't enough to capture the bathroom, and my stall was too small to move around and see beneath the others.

Steps echoed lightly, and I tried to quickly gather myself and flush. The sooner I could get back around the people in the main room, the better. I couldn't shake the dreadful feeling.

I turned from flushing the toilet and caught movement in the crack of the door. My eyes tried to focus, and I leaned in to catch a glimpse in the narrow view.

A woman moved into view, and I tripped back, steadying myself on the wall. In the blink of an eye, she was gone.

I unlocked the door quickly, her blood-covered appearance panicking me, urging me to help her. She knew my name.

Was it the woman from before, the one in the window?

The door flew open, and I was met with nothing. Not a single person stood in the bathroom, and silence hung in the air. Impossible.

She was there just a moment prior…

I rubbed my eyes, smudging my glitter eyeshadow a bit, and looked around again. No one was in the bathroom with me. I swallowed hard and approached the sink. The water ran freezing cold when I turned it on, and I let it splash against my skin, snapping me out of whatever delusion I was stuck in.

The lights flickered, and I tried to rinse the soap off faster. I couldn't grab a paper towel before the lights completely cut out. My heart stopped, and I sprinted for the door.

My hands scrambled against the wall in the dark, searching for it. I bumped into something and realized it was a trashcan as I maneuvered around it. A sound behind me made me move faster, and I nearly tumbled out into the hall as my hands found and pushed open the door.

I ran down the hall, back the way I came, without looking back. It wasn't until I was back up on the second floor that I paused to catch my breath and slow my heart rate.

What the fuck had I stepped into…

CHAPTER 14

I WANDERED the halls until I found one that looked vaguely familiar. After a few more minutes, I found the hall of rooms where the Wraith had left me. I poked my head inside the door, but he wasn't there waiting for me.

Instead of returning to the room, I slid down the wall beside the door and sat. Exhaustion swept over me after everything I experienced in a short few hours, the adrenaline crash real.

The events of the bathroom were still fresh in my mind, and I wasn't sure I wanted to be trapped in any room alone now, not without an easy escape. The woman disappeared; I never fully saw her, but I couldn't shake the feeling she had really been there.

Not a trick of my mind.

My arms wrapped around my knees and my eyes

felt heavy. I let my head fall a little, drooping until I stared at the floor. The plush carpeted halls were a deep red, the color of blood. I closed my eyes, trying to forget the bloody woman I'd seen.

My head bobbed and lifted suddenly. Had I nodded off waiting?

I shook my head and rubbed my eyes, trying to wake myself more. I wasn't built for partying through the night. Those days were well behind me.

Voices carried up the hall, and I tucked myself closer to the door, too tired to flee but not wanting to disrupt someone else's fun.

Perhaps it was the man I was waiting for; I couldn't leave if it was.

Two men rounded the corner, and neither was him. One was shorter, with sandy blond hair and a navy suit. The other was the exact opposite—dark features and an all-black ensemble.

They paused when they saw me seated on the ground, clearly not expecting anyone in this secluded corner of the house. The blonde man leaned in and whispered to the other before moving toward me.

I felt the urge to move away, too aware of how exposed I was on the floor alone.

"Are you okay?" the more jovial man asked.

"I'm good! Just waiting for someone," I admitted.

He gave a glance back to the other man, who had stopped walking.

"You look upset," he noted, turning back to me. "You should join us."

"Join?" I asked.

He grinned at me, and a shudder ran down my spine. "No one should be this displeased at Hollow House," he said, smiling gently at me.

He held out a hand and, skeptically, I took it.

The man behind him watched quietly, waiting patiently by the door he stopped in front of. His face read of a mixture of annoyance and defeat.

I knew I shouldn't go. The Wraith gave me a clear order: wait. Only hours before, I promised him I belonged to him for the night. What was I even thinking? That sounded like something out of one of the books Felix wrote.

This was real life. I got to make my decisions.

The flip flopping between my head and body was nauseating. One wanted to make its own decisions while the other wanted to wait for the touch of the man that made it come like no other.

Infuriating.

I decided to listen to my head, the often more reasonable of the two. I followed the man, realizing this could be the perfect opportunity to learn more.

So what if I had a bit of fun doing it too?

"I'm Ben," the blond said without any hesitation in his voice.

Maybe it was a fake name, but for some reason, I believed him when he said it.

"I thought there weren't names here," I stated.

He shrugged, and the other man eyed him, seemingly even more annoyed.

"For some, but not everyone follows every last rule," he said, his tone turning sultry. "He's Javier."

"Are you two—" I started.

Ben broke into laughter. The other man just continued his quiet walk into the room, sitting down on the bed in the middle.

"This is a house of desires," Ben said. "Titles don't matter here. Javier is helping me fulfill a desire, but he is not my partner."

My cheeks reddened, realizing the question was juvenile. Of course, couples here didn't really need to be together. The whole point was that anything was possible. Any desire could be fulfilled.

"Will you be joining us?" Ben asked, climbing into the bed next to Javier.

It all happened so quickly, I barely had time to realize I had to make a choice. I knew what I was accepting following them, but this all happened fast.

What did I expect? More conversation? That wasn't how things worked here.

The entire concept was going to make for great article material, though I'd have to omit some of the more private details of my night.

I walked forward and climbed into the bed, wordlessly accepting the offer. I needed a distraction before I lost my mind waiting around for the Wraith.

Javier and Ben wasted no time. Their hands wandered over me and pawed at my dress.

As the two men undressed me, I noticed a shadow in the doorway.

Hadn't we closed that?

I looked closer, the men oblivious to our new audience. My dress came completely off and my bra unhooked. The shadow moved, and with a bit of light pouring in from the hall, I made out the shape of a person.

Standing in the door was him, the man I'd hoped would come, and his eyes promised only darkness.

CHAPTER 15

My clothing was gone before I knew it, my gaze still on the man in the doorway. He didn't move, just continuing to watch. At some point, Ben and Javier took notice of him, but they dismissed it as the man fulfilling a voyeurism kink.

Neither seemed to care.

Javier pulled my hair away from my neck in a less-than-gentle tug, exposing my neck for him to kiss and nip. Ben moved to lie back on the bed and removed his pants, his large cock springing free. It was already fully erect, and I worried a bit as I took in the size.

He motioned for me to move, to get closer and climb on top of him.

Javier pulled away as I did and watched me position myself over Ben. The man grabbed my waist and guided me over his cock. In an instant, he had me impaled, the full size slamming into me in one go.

I winced and moaned, tipping my head back.

Javier moved behind me, his hands dancing along my skin. As I rode Ben, Javier massaged my bouncing tits with one hand and let the other flutter down to my clit. The new sensation sent my body into overdrive, but not enough to forget who watched.

"Look how good you take it," Ben demanded.

My eyes drifted down, and I forced them to remain open as I watched him slam into me. It hurt and sent shivers of pleasure through my body all at once, but not in the same way the Wraith had.

His cock barely fit, stretching me, surely leaving small tears.

I felt the eyes of the masked man in the corner watching me for what felt like hours. I wanted to look away and be in the moment, but his rich, dark eyes forced me to keep my gaze set on him instead of the two taking me.

My hand moved on instinct and reached out to him, beckoning him to me.

What was I doing?

I already had one man inside me and another running his hands along my body. Did I truly need another? My body craved his, unable to stay away. No matter how much I tried to focus on the other man pinning me to the bed, my only focus was the predator stalking toward me.

Another thrust into me had my gaze ripped away and back to Ben as I let out another moan.

"Eyes on me," the Wraith growled from across the room.

My head snapped back to him, and he closed the distance easily.

"Mine," he whispered, closing in on the man still pumping into me as I bounced in his lap.

I tried to move away, but Javier used his arm to keep me in place. The action almost possessive and without a thought for the third man approaching.

The Wraith didn't like that. He growled, grabbing the man by the collar of his shirt he'd managed to keep on. Javier fell backward, his mask falling crooked on his face.

I watched, unable to tear my eyes away and somehow still grinding on Ben's cock, the sheer possessive nature of the Wraith forcing my heart to race.

He came back for me.

As Javier backed away and stood in the doorway, it was clear he decided it was better not to fight the Wraith on this. Ben, however, had other ideas, even as I stopped my movements and climbed off him.

I hurried to the Wraith's side.

He moved to block Ben from me and pressed a kiss

to my lips, all in one swift motion. We were close to the wall, and he backed me into it, kissing me again and pressing me back, the cold sending a shiver down my spine.

"Hey, we weren't done here," Ben complained, putting a hand on the Wraith's shoulder.

My mind didn't have time to register what happened. He moved lightning fast. The Wraith grabbed Ben's hand as he pulled back from me, tugging it toward the wall and pulling out a blade with his other hand. Without as much as a flinch, the Wraith stabbed the knife straight through Ben's palm, pinning him to the wall.

Ben's cries of pain filled the room, and Javier fled. Blood dripped down the wall he was now pinned to. I let out a small yell, but the Wraith was back to me in an instant. He kissed me again, and I let him, frozen in… fear? Shock? I didn't know.

He pulled back after a few more seconds and brushed a strand of hair from my face.

"No one touches what is mine," he said.

I should hate it, the way he stabbed Ben and acted so possessive. But the second I heard the word *mine*, my core filled with heat, and I was helpless in his arms.

CHAPTER 16

I QUICKLY GRABBED and pulled my dress back on as we left the room and the Wraith led me to a new portion of the house.

"Here, drink this, love," the Wraith said, handing me a skeleton chalice.

Where'd he even grab that from?

I took it, needing to quench my thirst after everything I'd just done. I also needed it to forget the sight of the blade in Ben's hand.

I should've run the moment it happened, but I didn't, and I couldn't quite figure out why.

The Wraith held my hand, leading me up a set of stairs to a third floor and then a fourth I didn't know existed. It was tiny, a room the size of a closet acting as a landing. The only thing in the room was a door.

The window on the wooden door was made of

beautiful stained glass. I recognized the design worked into the glass, the same flower as the invite standing out.

I'd seen the same symbol throughout Hollow House.

"What is it?" I asked, and he followed my gaze to the flower.

"A rose," he stated, like it was obvious.

I mean it was, but I didn't understand how it fit into everything.

"It symbolizes respect. Most associate it with love, but here, it takes on new meaning."

I walked forward to see the details of the symbol better. It was an exact replica of my invite.

"Come, love. I want to show you something."

I blindly followed him, trusting him enough; he'd already had the chance to hurt me if he wanted to. Something inside me warred against that, especially after what he did to Ben. This was entirely unlike me. I always played it safe, followed the rules. What had changed inside me tonight that all that went out the window?

I played it safe in my work, stayed local after school, applied for the safe job, even avoided any type of uncomfortable conversations with friends and family. This was so far outside my comfort zone.

It had to be the drinks.

Whatever was in those skeleton chalices, I needed to be sure I grabbed the name of before the night was over. Anything strong enough to make me abandon every rule I set for myself was worth noting.

For avoidance in the future, of course.

The Wraith tugged open the door and led me out onto a small balcony. It was tucked high up in the front of the gothic mansion. From our position, I could see the entire town beneath me, the Halloween festivities dying out. I could barely make out any lights still on.

I knew most would take a glance at this house that sat on the hilly outskirts and wonder what was going on inside. Little did they know…

"Has Hollow House been to your liking?" the Wraith asked, surprising me.

I took a sip of my drink before answering. "It's definitely not what I expected," I answered truthfully.

"And what did you expect?" he asked raising a brow.

I walked over to the edge of the balcony and set my chalice down. I tried to spot my house from where I was and failed.

"An exaggerated party and a bunch of rich people." I shrugged.

"I'm sure there's some of that here, but not all of it," he mused, stepping closer.

He stood beside me, our bodies touching as we

looked out to the town together. We stayed like that in silence for a few minutes before he spoke again.

"I want you to join our Hollow Society," the Wraith said.

I searched his face for any hint that he was joking. The words that left his mouth made no sense. I'd known him hours, barely had a conversation with him, and now…

"I know you, Sloane," he said, reading my mind. "It's why I picked you. You've been cast out by society, passed up for every opportunity. You have no one in your corner."

That wasn't true. I had Felix, and—I paused, realizing that was it. My parents and I barely spoke anymore. They'd moved on from the small town, whereas I stayed trapped. Felix was my sole friend. I didn't have siblings or any coworkers I enjoyed.

"I—" I started but stopped. "Felix is my friend."

It was all I could think to say. My cheeks warmed, embarrassed by how secluded I'd let myself become with my work. Felix had his own life now. He would always be my best friend, but he had a partner now, amazing writing opportunities. Even the sex toy shop was a part of all that.

"Join us," the Wraith offered again. "We can be everything you crave, every desire you've ever had…"

"What do you know of my every desire?" I

snapped, throwing my hands over my mouth, unable to stop the words.

The Wraith barely flinched. Instead, a wicked grin curled his lips. "I know you work at the local magazine. I know you've never once been offered a promotion or new opportunities. You get passed over for the ones who suck off their boss. I know the pig you work under. I know you wish to leave this town, to make it big, work for the top magazines. We can give you that. Anything you desire will be yours if you accept."

"I don't understand," I said, the words barely a whisper. Not a single thing he said was false.

"How do you think the wealthy and powerful get where they are?" he asked.

"Nepotism," I scoffed.

He let out a gentle laugh and pulled me closer to his body. The heat of him pressed against me, providing the perfect balance to the cool night air. I took a deep breathe, his scent something like bourbon. It was inviting, something I wanted to stay wrapped in.

"That is certainly one way, but there are other ways too. Powerful people pull strings. They work to put people in positions that serve them."

"Are you saying that's what you do?" I asked, spinning to face him, my brows raised.

Shit. If that were true, this was it. This was the

single piece of information I needed to make sure my article was my way out.

"Those with power need lawyers, politicians, agents, journalists…" He trailed off, his eyes shifting from the town beneath us to me. Even in the dark, I could see him perfectly. His dark eyes settled on me, and I almost lost my train of thought.

"People like me make that happen," he said. "I'm a ghost to the world, a shadow pulling the strings of power."

"I barely know you. Why me? Why, after mere hours, are you offering all this to me?" I asked, a sinking feeling filling me as I suspected his answer.

"Because I've been watching you far longer than those hours," he said.

A lump formed in my throat. All those times I felt watched …

"It was you in the bar?" I asked, and he nodded. "And in my house?"

He didn't move, but his eyes gave him away. I backed away from him, taking him in fully. The man I'd spent my entire night with had been stalking me?

"It's my job. I'm a shadow. I find those society gave up on, who deserve a shot at greatness," he said.

I shook my head, unable to process it.

"Join us," he offered, holding out his hand to join him at the edge.

I swallowed hard, weighing the option. If I took it, could he really give me a way out? It was what I yearned for and worked my ass off to find. It never came easy, and still, I hadn't found that big break.

This could be it.

I knew I should take it. My boss would never actually give me what I wanted. He didn't even have faith in me to write the article I promised—the article I now had all the information I needed for.

I hesitated, and the Wraith watched me with such intensity, I took a step back.

"I think I should go…" I started.

I hate the words the second they left my mouth, each one like poison on my tongue. The look of hurt that flashed across his face only made it worse. I didn't want to disappoint him, but I barely knew him.

"Sloane," he started.

"Just let me go," I interrupted, not strong enough to put up a fight if he argued for me to stay.

Before he could stop me, I turned and ran.

CHAPTER 17

I MIRACULOUSLY FOUND my way back to the front entry and out the door. The gravel driveway crunched beneath my heels as I sprinted toward the gate. Two men outside leaned against the stone column on one side of the steps. I paid them little attention, just wanting to leave.

My mistake.

They moved, following behind me at an unhurried pace. Did they come from inside the party? They wore the same masks as everyone else, but they weren't inside. Did they slip through the gates and end up locked out with no invite?

I tried not to let my mind wander to the worst thoughts as I slowed my pace and stopped at the gate.

I tugged on it, but it barely budged. The more I

pulled, the more my panic grew. The footsteps behind me were close, and my stomach sank.

Was I locked in?

I turned to face the approaching men, taking a few steps away from the gate, my hands on my hips.

"What?" I snapped at the pair.

"We were just wondering where you're heading so soon into the night?" one of the men with red hair asked. The other stood beside him, his long blond hair pulled back.

"I'm leaving," I said firmly.

They both laughed.

"You hear that, John?" the red haired one asked.

"I did, Greg. Maybe we can convince her otherwise."

"Just one small taste of this," Greg said and reached out to grab my ass.

I swatted his hand away, and he gave me an undignified look. The guy was deranged. His hair was swept all over the place, his mask crooked. I knew the alcohol served here was strong, but this strong? Enough to justify such lack of judgement? I don't think so.

Fucking creep.

"Go the fuck back inside," I said, trying to inject some confidence into the statement.

He laughed—fucking *laughed*—right in my face.

The nerve of this guy. I could feel the jackass' ego oozing from him. Such an entitled prick.

I turned to storm back toward the gate, and he reached out, grabbing my waist. Why I thought turning away from him was a good idea, I have no idea, but apparently, I was full of bad ideas tonight.

"Let's go, princess," he said.

"I'm not your fucking princess," I said, trying to kick him away as he literally dragged me by my waist.

I cursed under my breath, one of his muscular arms thicker than both my arms combined. The man was a beast, one I had no hope of escaping from. Whatever he wanted, it was probably better to let him have it without a fight and then get the fuck out of there.

My body gave up, my tense muscles going limp, and I whimpered as the guy pulled my hair. He wrapped it around his hand and tugged on it like a leash.

My cries were mangled and soft, my head forced to face the ground and my feet skidding across gravel.

I tried to minimize the pain. My hands went to my scalp and tried to prevent any pieces of hair from ripping out with his aggression as I heard the other man let out a laugh.

The laugh turned into something far stranger, more of a muffled cry. I tried to glance up, but the man shoved my face back down. Footsteps crunched on the ground, and I no longer heard the other one.

The tight grip on my hair loosened for a second, and I pulled back, distancing myself from the man as he lost his hold.

When I looked up, I noticed one man passed out on the ground. What the fuck?

My head spun, finding someone dragging the other across the driveway. I recognized the black suit.

The Wraith pulled him into a headlock and cut off his air until he was helpless. I'd never seen such raw strength from someone.

He passed out, and the Wraith dropped him like he was nothing. The body hit the ground with a hard thud, and all I could do was watch.

"Apologies, love," the Wraith cooed, stepping over the body. "It would seem some of those in Hollow Society have completely lost their manners. They will be dealt with."

"Don't hurt them," I blurted out before I could stop it.

His brow ticked up in surprise. "I promise, they will not be harmed," he said and held out a hand.

I don't know why I did it, but this time, I took it without hesitation. Maybe it was because the gate was locked and I knew it was useless until morning, or maybe it was the way he'd protected me without hesitation. I didn't know.

I tried not to overthink it. Besides, I had a job to finish. If I didn't get some form of an article out of the night, it would all be for nothing.

Before heading back inside, I caught a glimpse of the balcony above, two men watching me with intense stares I could feel even behind their masks. I lost sight of them the second I walked up the front steps, but something about them felt almost familiar…

CHAPTER 18

"Are you okay?" the Wraith asked the second we were inside.

He glanced me over like he was looking for injuries, and I stood frozen in shock. The sudden attention and care was too much.

"Why do you care?" I asked with a sigh of defeat.

I'd given in, went back inside, but part of me still wanted to run, to be done with this assignment. To write an article that exposed the place for what it was....

A house of horrors, not pleasures.

The place had a way of making you slowly lose your mind. All night long, I couldn't tell what was reality and what was my mind playing tricks. The woman in the window, the one in the bathroom—was any of it real?

"Are you even real?" I asked without realizing I said it out loud until his brows raised.

He moved closer, and my feet remained firmly planted. If this wasn't reality, what did I care if he was in my space? Maybe this was all a dream, and I'd wake back in my bed.

He reached for my hand slowly, watching me for any sign of denial, but I let him continue. It landed on his chest, and I could feel his heart beating steadily beneath my touch.

"This is real, love," he promised. "Take a few deep breaths."

I tried inhaling and exhaling to the same rhythm as the rise and fall of his chest. Eventually, the sheer panic that had grabbed me so forcefully resided. He watched me, never once letting go of my hand.

"Sorry," I muttered.

"Don't be," he insisted. "There's nothing wrong with asking questions."

I looked up and found his dark eyes glancing me over. My gaze dropped to his lips, and before I could change my mind, I stood on my toes and kissed him.

His hands moved to my face to hold me there, but after a second, he backed away.

"Let's go somewhere with fewer watchful eyes this time," he said, leading me back inside.

It wasn't until we reached a new door in a hall I

wasn't sure I had been in that we paused. He opened the door, letting me in first.

The room was filled with mirrors and padded floors, a gym turned into a room of various desires. I spotted brand new vibrators still in their packages, bondage, even paddles.

"Tell me, love: which do you desire?"

The words tickled my ear on his whisper. I glanced around, but nothing specific caught my eye. Only a few hours in, I wasn't sure if I wanted the Wraith to use some of the more unfamiliar toys just yet. Nerves crept through my body, self-consciousness at the fact that he was likely far more experienced.

He saw the way my arms wrapped around my middle and I shied away from him. His arms wrapped around me and tucked me close. "Let's start with the familiar," he said. "A simple game."

"A game?"

"For each question asked, we remove a piece of clothing," he mused.

"I'm pretty sure that's not how that game goes," I answered, a smile tugging at my lips. I expected far worse.

He shrugged.

"Maybe I'm just trying to find an excuse to see you without clothing again."

"I'll play," I said.

I crossed the room and picked up a tickler. When I spun back to face him, he had closed a bit of distance between us. I pointed the tickler at him. "You first."

"Fine. What's your favorite color?" he asked with a smirk.

I saw exactly what he was doing, and I wouldn't make it so easy for him.

"Pink," I said, tossing my pink-streaked hair behind my shoulder.

I reached down and pulled off my pair of black heels. My feet were aching, pulsing with freedom the second they went flat. My arms crossed and hip popped as I gave him a wicked grin.

"What's your name?" I asked.

He took a step closer.

"Damon," he answered without hesitation, slipping off the black loafers he wore.

This game wouldn't last long. It was far too easy, and there were minimal layers I had to work with. But I didn't care. That was the point.

"Why do you truly wish to write an article on Hollow House?" he asked.

"I thought you would know that," I pointed out.

"Humor me, love," he said.

"I want a promotion," I answered and shrugged.

It was at least part of the truth, but his eyes bore into me like he saw past that tidbit of information. The silence burned through me as I slipped my hand to pull off my bra.

"Not yet," he stopped me with two words.

I let go of my dress and stopped fidgeting with the fabric. My head cocked, waiting for him to elaborate.

"Answer fully, or you didn't answer," he said.

"I did—"

"You didn't, or you're lying to yourself. You don't want to be stuck at that small town magazine," he said.

He saw right through me. He'd claimed to know all about me; apparently, that stalking was intricate and thorough. Beyond just my job, he knew details of my life few knew.

"Fine," I admitted. "I want my ticket away from here."

I maneuvered my dress and slowly, tortuously, pulled off my bra, keeping my eyes set on him. His entire body tensed; I could tell he was holding himself back. Only steps away from him, I reached out with the tickler, running the feathers along his neck. The shudder that ran through his body was visible.

I wasn't even quite sure I was using the thing right, but it seemed to have an effect on him, which was my goal.

"What is your deepest desire?" I asked.

Another step closer, and I knew only one more would close the gap between us.

"To make you mine," he said as he closed the last step and unbuttoned his shirt, tossing it to the side. His arms wrapped around my waist and tugged at my dress.

"Take this off," he demanded, done with the questions and turning impatient.

"I thought we were getting to know each other a bit," I teased.

"I know enough, and now, I know I need this," he said, sliding a hand down to cup my ass. "There will be plenty of time for other questions eventually."

I tried to ignore what that inferred and how it made my heart leap. He wanted to see me more than just this, maybe even after Halloween ended. I chose not to analyze it as he guided me over to the bench in the room, sitting down on it. His hands tugged at me, my ass backing into him. I was completely exposed as he unhooked my bra and tossed it aside.

My cheeks warmed, catching sight of us in one of the many mirrors around the room.

"Watch how fucking beautiful you are," he said as I sat back against him and he slipped his fingers into me.

He wrapped a strong arm around me, and my hands immediately grabbed him. I was sitting in his lap instead of the bench, and in the mirror across from the bench, I saw us.

His eyes were glued to it, watching the way I

reacted to every touch and movement. My cheeks flushed, seeing how intense his stare was on my body.

I could see everything. My entire pussy was on display.

I tipped my head back against the Wraith, but his other hand grabbed my chin and forced me back to watching.

"I want you to watch as I make you come," he ordered. "I need to see you scream my name before I make those wicked lips suck my cock."

I didn't last long beyond that, shocked my body still had any orgasms left in it. Was this some new record or something?

At what point did the human body shut down from pleasure?

My ass pressed back into his hardened dick, and my mouth watered, wanting to taste him.

His fingers continued to make quick work of me, and soon, I spilled over the edge. I screamed his name as the orgasm slammed into me and my body trembled. I barely held myself up, his strong arms the only thing saving me.

Before I could even process it, he flipped me around and lifted me. My legs wrapped around him to help hold myself up as he walked me into one of the mirrored walls. The glass was cold against my naked body, and I feared I may break something. Damon wasn't gentle, and my heart raced, terrified the glass would shatter.

He pulled his cock from his pants and easily slipped inside me.

His thrusts were hard, and I clung as close to his body as I could. The friction of our skin pressed together and my clit rubbing against him had me shuddering.

I let my legs drop from his hips after a moment, and he pulled out of me. I dropped to the floor and slowly moved him to place his back to the wall.

His eyes questioned me, brows raised, but he didn't stop me.

I dropped to my knees in front of him, to fulfill his desire. My hands wrapped around his cock and guided it to my mouth. At first, it was a lot, maybe too much. His dick barely fit and I gagged. He hit the back of my throat as I took him in. It took a few thrusts before I found a good rhythm. Tears lined my eyes just from his sheer size.

He gripped my hair, using his leverage to help push the pace. As his dick slipped in and out of my mouth, I dragged my tongue up the shaft. He let out a deep moan, and his fingers tightened their grip.

I could taste his pre cum as he prepared to topple over the edge. I knew it was coming. His entire body tensed, and his thrusts became faster. His head tipped back as he released, cum dripping down my throat.

"Fuck," he moaned as he finished.

I pulled back and wiped my mouth on my arm. When I glanced up, I found him staring down at me, watching, taking in my every move.

He stepped around me and walked toward the bench, collecting our clothing. He pulled on his shirt and secured the buttons in place once more. I slipped the dress back on, leaving my bra off.

He sat on the floor and leaned against the mirrors, beckoning for me to join. I tucked myself beside him and let myself slip down to rest.

We stayed silent, resting for what felt like hours. My body was growing even more tired but clinging to what I had found at Hollow House. I no longer wanted to run. I didn't want to return to my house empty-handed.

My head rested on his lap as I laid there, curled up on the floor beside him.

A familiar beep sounded from his pocket, and I lifted my head off his lap. My eyes alternated between watching him play with my hair in the mirror to shut for a few minutes. Sleep was calling for me, but the night wasn't over. Dawn was approaching soon, and I dreaded it.

I sat up, letting him pull out his phone.

"I have to deal with one more thing," he said and lightly kissed my forehead.

"Don't leave me here," I blurted and slapped a hand over my mouth, embarrassed at how quickly I let myself get attached.

It was a night.

Tomorrow, things would be different.

Felix was wrong. I didn't need a hook up. I needed my therapist and to swear off hook ups for another year. But again, maybe losing touch with who I was could be good for me. It was uncomfortable at first, but once I worked through whatever this need was, it could be okay.

"It'll only be twenty minutes," he promised. "Why don't you explore the rest of the halls on this side of the mansion?"

Wandering had landed me in plenty of trouble before.

"For your article, of course," he said with a mischievous grin.

Now, I really couldn't say no.

CHAPTER 19

After the Wraith, Damon, left again and another waiter passed a drink off to me, I found myself standing in a new hall. It was one I had not been to yet, darker than the rest. This section of the house was far removed. It led to a single door at the end, and curiosity won me over, every other portion of the house a work of art.

I let myself wander to the only door and push it open. He said to help myself to the house, and I certainly was. Although, I imagine he meant the party still going on elsewhere. Or perhaps it ended—I hadn't passed it and couldn't hear the music any longer.

It didn't matter.

The second I stepped inside, I realized it was an office, the large desk covered in papers, shelves lined with books gave it away.

It was straight out of a movie.

It certainly beat my old, beat up plastic desk as home. This belonged to someone important, someone of standing, not some measly journalist.

The Wraith claimed to be just that.

And he was serious…

Pictures hung all over the walls of every imaginable influential person—politicians I recognized, men in expensive business suits, women with more power than I would ever have, all standing with the same person.

Damon.

I didn't recognize him. I hadn't seen his face all night, but even like this, in a normal setting, I had no idea who he was.

The puppet master, the one pulling the strings, the person controlling this version of society.

A small sound behind me caught my attention, and I turned to find nothing.

I turned my focus back to the pictures, dismissing it as noises in the hall.

I set my cup down and glanced over every single picture, some with articles and awards next to them. He'd swayed elections, helped secure accolades for major actors, and even held favor with men on Wall Street.

Another sound, and this time, I froze. It was closer. *Louder.*

Floorboards creaking beneath someone's feet. I turned around, sure I would find Damon, but no one was there. My body refused to move for a few seconds until I found my courage again. I twisted back to the wall but felt a small chill down the right side of my body.

I let my head turn slightly and spotted nothing but a crooked frame.

I squinted, spotting a woman in the photo and instantly recognizing her: the person I had idolized for years. She owned the largest magazine in New York City. How could I not recognize her?

I pulled the tiny frame off the wall for a better look, to make sure my eyes were not deceiving me.

"I had a feeling I would find you here, love," Damon crooned.

I turned, dropping the photo in my hands, completely startled. Stunned wasn't even the best way to describe how I felt. Overwhelmed, in denial, perplexed…those all came close, but it still wasn't enough.

I shook my head as my heart settled from the scare the second my eyes landed on him.

There was nothing to be afraid of with him. This was his house. No one would be allowed to harm me, and there likely weren't any actual threats out there, just a combination of exhaustion and being tipsy that kept my mind active and overthinking every little sound.

"How did you know?" I asked, trying to focus on something else.

"A dear friend mentioned they saw you heading in this direction," he answered.

The waiter.

It had to be—who else would have even noticed me? Maybe others were watching closer than I thought.

"Have you finished with whatever called you off?" I asked.

"I have," he answered with a slight nod.

My hands drifted behind my back, clasped together. I glanced to him with hooded eyes, imagining every way we could make use of this office.

He let out a chuckle that warmed me.

"Patience, love," he answered. "I have one last place I want to show you before the night ends," he said, holding out his hand.

CHAPTER 20

Each time I thought I had seen the entirety of the house, a new hallway appeared, a labyrinth rather than a mansion. Damon gave my hand a firm squeeze as we turned down the new one. He opened one of the doors and stepped aside to let me in first.

A throne sat in the middle of the room, and I froze in the doorway, barely able to believe my eyes. If I hadn't encountered far stranger all night, I would've surely believed myself drugged.

Damon nudged me forward, his massive frame filling the doorway behind me.

"What is this?" I asked, turning into him, my hands landing on his chest.

"For you," is all he said.

I turned my head to glance back at the throne, but

before I could take it in, to see if I'd imagined it, his hand caught my chin and turned me back.

The way he gripped my face was sure to leave bruises, a thought that should terrify me, but I found I wasn't scared.

Not with him.

This house of desires and nightmares had my heart racing, but the second he was by my side, I felt oddly safe.

Yup, I was truly going mad.

I tried to extricate myself from his grip, curiosity burning hot in my chest. This time, he grabbed my hips and flipped me around without warning, pressing me back to him.

My eyes took in the throne in its entirety, sitting in the center of an otherwise-empty room. The black and gold matched most of the décor throughout the mansion.

I had to blink a few times just to be sure I wasn't hallucinating. It wouldn't be the first time tonight, and I was starting to feel like it might not be the last.

"Why is this here? This can't seriously be for me?" I asked.

"It wasn't originally brought here for you specifically, but rather, for the woman of my desires."

I almost choked at his words, holding back a giggle. I looked back, only to find him completely serious.

Moonlight poured in from the single window, almost spotlighting the chair. I walked toward it, drawn to it for some reason, its presence both magnetic and unsettling. The air in the room weighed on me, and I held my breath, not knowing what I was even waiting for.

My hand ran along the arm of the throne, an intricate golden metal design. The seat itself was black with a tall back, outlined in gold.

"Sit," he commanded from behind me, his voice growing closer.

My pulse picked up, and I slid into the chair, which felt massive compared to my tiny frame. An odd hum rang in my ears as I watched him approach. It grew louder, only adding to the blood rushing in my ears. My head spun as he leaned over me, arms on either side, gripping the arm rests.

"Perfection," he said in a low tone.

I swallowed hard. The word shouldn't have made me flush the way I did. This house of pleasure was one whole night of purely ludicrous happenings.

"This is ridiculous," I huffed.

"Is it?" he asked, leaning in further and pressing kisses to my neck. "Is this whole house not a tad ridiculous then, this entire party, a house of pleasures? Some might say that is also a little ridiculous, and yet, you're still here. So perhaps it is the rest of the world who places the unexpected into ridiculous little boxes and tries to trap us there?"

"Damon…" I started as he resumed his nips and kisses.

"Do you feel it?" he asked.

"Feel what?" I responded.

He dragged a hand slowly up my thigh, eyes now locked on mine. "The way people here respond to you, the way you fit perfectly in this house," he answered.

Before I could answer, he leaned back in and cut off my words, gently kissing my lips. He pulled back slightly, his words a whisper against my flesh.

"You belong here," he said firmly.

The chill in the room intensified, the humming growing louder. Goosebumps spread across my arms, and I shivered under his touch.

"Damon, I can't---" I started, unsure what I even wanted to say.

My head swam with every possible thought. This was not what I was expecting to find when I decided to come here. I never once thought this entire new future would be laid out before me. A single article, that was all this was supposed to be. A way to get Darren off my back. And now what? Damon wanted me to give up my life for one I had only seen a glimpse of in a single night.

Damon pulled away completely and held out a

hand as my head still tried to wrap itself around the offer that hung between us.

"Come. The party is almost over."

CHAPTER 21

THE BALLROOM-SIZED ROOM I had started off in was silent when we entered. Men and women in their masks gathered in the middle, but not a single one spoke. They just parted to let us pass.

The music had ended and the DJ was gone.

I didn't spot any of the waiters from before, realizing the crowd had formed a circle of sorts in the middle of the room. Damon was leading me to the middle.

He stopped at the edge, encouraging me forward. I hated all the eyes on me. It was different when it was just him, but now, I realized there were at least fifty or more people here, all with their focus trained on me.

The ballroom was darker than before, the lights dimmed, curtains drawn shut. The chandelier above was the only reason I could make out anyone around me. I still couldn't gather many details of their appearances, their masks still firmly in place.

My skin crawled, each stare tearing into me. The way Damon saw through me, could they also?

Movement in the crowd caught my attention as they parted for someone new. Bodies shifted to let whoever it was pass. I couldn't make them out until they stood in front of me. The hole in the circle closed, and I studied them.

A man much taller than me stood across the circle, his gaze on the ground and something familiar in his hands. The same blade from earlier in the night. I recognized the strange, long handle.

My eyes were too focused on the blade to notice when the man in front of me pulled off his mask. He walked toward me, and I refused to lift my eyes, afraid to lose track of the weapon.

Was this it?

Was it all an elaborate plan to kill me?

The blade lifted in front of me, and I tensed, readying myself for the blow. Surrounded by the circle of people, I had nowhere to run. I had nothing to help me fight back. I was helpless.

The blade paused at my chest.

"Take it," a familiar voice said.

I looked up, and my jaw completely dropped.

"Felix?" I asked, watching my best friend step forward.

He walked toward me without a word. Instead, he continued to hold out the knife.

I tried to reach out to my friend, desperate for an explanation, but he walked away. His eyes refused to meet mine as he looked to the Wraith for approval.

The book deals, the job at the sex toy shop that supplied this place, even his mysterious partner from out of town…it was all adding up. The signs were there, I just didn't see them.

That was how the Wraith knew who I was before I came. The strange change in attitude Felix had before I came tonight made far more sense. He knew exactly what I was walking into.

My mouth opened, but the Wraith held up a hand, stopping me.

Instead, he motioned across from me, and the crowd parted. Someone dragged a man forward, his hands cuffed and a bag over his head.

I could hear muffled curses from under it, but I couldn't make out much more.

"Choose," the Wraith said, and I knew what he meant. "Will the pedophile live or die?"

His voice was firm, but again, I wasn't afraid. After all the chances he had to hurt me, to kill me if he wanted, I did not fear him. Rather, I feared myself, what he wanted me to do. I couldn't hurt any innocent man…

But the last thing he said caught in my head.

Pedophile?

Someone pulled the bag from his head. The man looked around, panicked, before his gaze settled on me and the knife in my hand.

My entire body trembled, barely registering him. It wasn't until he cursed again that I recognized his voice. My vision cleared, and I focused on him better.

Darren.

My boss stood across from me, anger spreading across his face. He tugged at the cuffs on his wrists without any success.

"You bitch," he growled. "This is where you've been? Partying instead of working?"

He knew I was writing this article and what that meant. Why was the bastard acting surprised?

I glanced at the man across from me, a truly vile and disgusting person. The world would be a far better place if he were no longer in it. I closed my eyes and pictured all the women who would be safer without him around. How many had he successfully assaulted, who hadn't pushed back the way I did? How many had sacrificed something so precious to them just to keep their job?

The thought had bile rising in my throat.

I opened my eyes, this time narrowed onto him. The asshole didn't even have the decency to look concerned. Instead, he stood with a smug grin on his face, watching me.

"Pedophile?" I questioned, looking from him to Damon.

"He has multiple allegations against him," Damon stated.

I knew by the look in his eyes, I would not be getting more information. This was about testing loyalty, proving my worth to the Society, proving I would do whatever must be done to be a part of it.

"None of them ever proven," Darren scoffed. The bastard had the audacity to grin as he said it. I knew they weren't just allegations…

"You seriously think she's going to kill me?" he laughed the question at the Wraith. "She can barely write an article, never mind be an obedient worker. I doubt she'd listen to your nonsense, not if she knows what's best for her."

His gaze settled on me with such hunger, I realized I was utterly fucked if he survived. His eyes promised punishment if I ever stepped foot in the office again. Forget the article on Hollow House—I was out of a job regardless.

I sucked in a deep breath and held it, trying to figure out a way out of it all, one that didn't make me a murderer and allowed me to keep my position. Without it, I was nothing, and I would never make my way out of the small town.

"You're right," I admitted, looking at my boss.

His smug features made my insides curl. If I could run away and never see the asshole again, I would have long before.

"You've known me years, and I follow every last rule. I take every assignment and follow the instructions. I have never once stepped out of line," I said.

The more satisfaction spread on his face, the worse I felt. I hated watching him win. The hold he had on me was inescapable.

I stepped forward a couple feet, the space between us minimal. My eyes met his, and I tried to search for any form of a human behind them, anything forgivable, redeemable even. Could he change? Could I still work for him?

"I certainly never would kill someone," I spoke again, and out of the corner of my eye, I saw Damon.

His features didn't change, but I knew he was watching intensely, waiting for me to make a choice. The choice was simple: kill him and join or walk away.

Would they even allow me to walk away?

I couldn't publish an article with this. My entire way out was fucked. There was barely anything I could work with without incriminating myself now. What would they even do with Darren? Let him go? Or kill him to keep their secret?

"You're going nowhere," Darren spat. "When you get back, I will be evaluating your performance again. Perhaps this time, I'll fire you. And you won't do a thing about it, because I know you."

I took that last step between us. "You knew me, but I no longer recognize myself," I spoke before I drove the knife into his heart.

CHAPTER 22

SHE SLAMMED the knife into his chest, and I watched with pride as he stumbled back.

She was mine for eternity.

Damned like the rest of us.

Cast out from society, banding together in our own little world.

She belonged to me now.

Her eyes filled with horror at the realization of what she'd done.

Before the rest could see her, I stepped in. My hands cupped her face, and I forced her gaze to me. Dropping my hands, I gripped the handle of the knife and pulled it from her grasp. She didn't fight me. My lips collided with hers then, kissing away any hesitation or regret she had building inside her. I let my tongue drift along the outside of her lips, searching for an invitation.

The rest of the room left, leaving her as all mine to devour.

CHAPTER 23

The Wraith kissed me hard. At some point, he'd ordered everyone out of the room, but I was too numb to notice. My entire body felt like pins and needles were jabbing into me. Thoughts raced through my mind, but none were coherent.

At some point, my knees buckled and the only thing holding me up was him. He lowered me safely to the floor, pulling back from the kiss.

My eyes stung with tears, and I could barely see him. Blood stained the ground beneath me, and I tried not to let my gaze drop, but I failed.

"Love," the Wraith said. His voice pulled my stare up, like a siren beckoning me into his grasp. I was helpless against his pull. "Don't cry for him," he said. "He was a predator."

"I know," I managed to choke out.

"Let me help you forget," he said. "Let me distract you until the pain and memory fades away."

I didn't know what to do or say. No one forced that knife into my hands. Not a single person in the room made me stab him.

I'd done that all on my own.

Maybe I was as terrible as the rest of them.

"We should call for help, save him," I said, a spark of reason snapping me out of my state.

"He's gone now," the Wraith said. He reached out, pulling me into his lap, and I curled into his body.

Our lips collided again in a mess of kisses. Tears still fell down my face, and I knew they streaked his face from proximity. I tried not to think about it, not to feel, but I failed miserably. I felt everything.

He lowered me down and pulled back to watch my face for approval. I knew I shouldn't; this entire night was fucked, but what was one more thing when my morality was completely gone? I nodded, needing something more.

My back pressed into something wet, but all I could focus on was the man above me.

He unzipped his pants and pulled out his cock. I tensed, already anticipating its entrance. At first, he was slow, almost hesitant. His eyes watched me for any sense of regret, waiting for me to pull away.

Would he kill me too if I did?

My mind raced back to the rooftop, to what he said. Those who stayed with him found their success, their deepest desires.

That was everything I searched for, everything I had been working toward, the dream I continually grasped for and never seemed to reach, that Darren kept me from. This was it.

All I had to do was accept what he was offering.

A spot with him…with the rest of the Hollow Society. Those who had everything ripped from them by the world. Those who had become hollow inside, desperate enough to do anything to escape the pit they were slipping into.

I felt that darkness pulling me down.

He devoured me in a single thrust, his cock pushing inside me until I felt myself arching into him. My head tipped back against the hard floor. This wasn't the same lust-filled sex as before. It wasn't gentle or caring. It was completely primal.

My hands reached for him, landing on his hardened abdominal muscles. I let them wander along them, tracing his tattoos. A skull sat in the center of them all, staring back at me. I was damned.

Pain rushed through me as I felt him stretch my pussy, my wetness doing little to help how large his dick was. With everything that happened, there wasn't enough foreplay to even be considerably wet.

Still, I felt myself unraveling beneath him.

With each thrust, I lost a bit more of myself, the person I was no longer an option. I forged a new path for myself, one where I was selfish and chose myself over everything.

He slipped off and moved to lie beside me.

His strong arms moved me to sit on top of him. I positioned his cock at my entrance as I had before and let myself slip down onto it. The pain of the hard floor against my knees was welcomed.

My mind wandered, thinking back to everything the night was. Every little brush and touch of skin, every kiss, every moment like this. Each was met with something unexplainable. Maybe this place was haunted, the stories kids told to explain the house on the hill all true. The people I had seen, presences felt— how else could I explain that? How many lives had been taken here?

Damon walked me into a room a few away from the room we'd been in. I watched people rush by us dressed in hazmat suits to clean up the mess I made, the one I couldn't walk away from now.

"Stop thinking about them," he demanded, grabbing my hand and squeezing. "You have nothing to regret here. You did what was right."

What was right…

Right for who? Myself? I still tried to grapple with it all.

In the new room, the same people crowded around from before, but this time, something was different. They no longer wore their masks. They watched us enter, all smiling and giving nods of approval. Before, they barely even flashed a smile at me.

I spotted Felix and Jeremy in the corner, whispering to each other and holding similar chalices to what had been served all night. The couple up on the balcony before, now I knew why they felt so familiar. I did know them. My best friend and his partner, dressed in clothing fancier than anything I ever seen them in, mingling with a secret society.

A secret society I was now a part of. I damned myself to this; I needed to learn to accept it. If I wanted to move on and make something of myself, I couldn't let fear and regret hold me back, not when I knew there was more for me beyond where I'd become stuck.

I just couldn't shake the terrible sinking feeling in my gut that followed stabbing Darren. He was a horrible person. I heard some of the accusations against him at work that HR did nothing about. He deserved the karma that found him.

But still, I had to live with what I did.

I decided what his punishment should be. I let the society sink their claws in and push me toward this. There was no backing out now.

I stopped following Damon's lead. He stopped and looked back, tilting his head out of concern. His strong grip tightened, and the squeeze was enough to pull me out of the spiral I was aiming for.

People started to approach and congratulate me. Their words barely registered. Instead, my focus was stuck on my friend who had not come over yet. He was avoiding me, and I wanted to know why.

After a few more introductions and pleasantries, I turned to Damon, leaning in so no one else could over-hear me.

"Will you excuse me for a second?" I whispered to him.

"Of course," he said, his tone dark.

I walked over to Felix, my friend's partner leaving his side to let the two of us talk.

"He's taken a special interest in you. He never does that," Felix said before I could even speak..

"What do you mean?"

"He doesn't let people as close to him as he has you."

"It's been one night, Felix. It was a single night of hook ups. I'm sure he's had others," I said.

"Sloane, it's been almost a month."

My entire world crashed around me. Reality bent, and I felt sick. My hands grabbed my stomach and mouth while I tried to hold back the bile rising in my throat. I dry heaved, and Felix tried to put a hand on my back, which I quickly swatted away.

"You left me here that long? How is that even possible? It's only been a night," I said, scrambling for an explanation.

"You saw me here, Sloane. We talked," he said, his eyes searching mine.

"What?" I asked, but as he said it, I remembered. The dream. I thought it was all a fantasy, that Felix couldn't really be there…

But it wasn't. It wasn't just a trick of my mind or too much wine. I was truly losing touch with reality.

"Are you okay?" he asked, watching me spiral.

"No, I'm not okay," I yelled. "My best friend, who I thought I could trust, was a part of this all along."

"I never wanted to lie to you," he said.

"Did you kill someone?"

He dropped his head, refusing to meet my gaze. "Yes."

My mouth fell open. The man I'd known since

kindergarten, who wrote books about fairies and true love, was now a killer—and I was too.

I looked at my bloodstained hands. Why didn't the sight repulse me? Why no matter how hard I tried, did I not instantly regret it? Why did I still want him?

"Was any of it real?" I asked.

I wasn't sure if I meant our friendship or Hollow House or my whole damn reality.

"Of course," he said, rushing forward and pulling me into hug. "I'm still your best friend. I'm sorry I kept this from you. It was for your own good. If I told you anything, you wouldn't be allowed to join. You had to decide on your own."

Decide.

That was what I had done. I'd made a choice, one that could have monumentally fucked me over.

My body was numb, the will to push Felix away gone. It barely registered as he continued, rambling about the Hollow Society and his place in it. My mind and gaze were only focused on one thing across the room.

Him.

Was it all a dream, was I dead, or did I just damn myself for eternity?

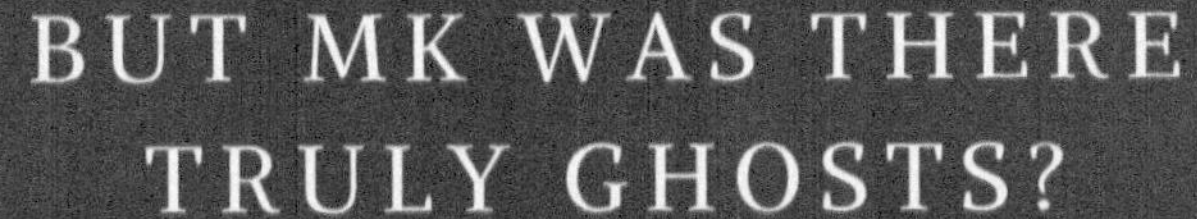

BUT MK WAS THERE
TRULY GHOSTS?

I SUPPOSE THAT
DEPENDS ON IF YOU
BELIEVE IN THEM...

ACKNOWLEDGMENTS

Every time I sit down to write these acknowledgments, I am so emotional thinking about everyone who made this all possible.

To my family, thank you for your endless support and for still cheering me on even when the mile long trigger warning list terrified you!

To my husband, thank you for listening to me think through the ending scene and never once judging me for my twisted ideas.

To my editor, Alexa, YOU DESERVE THE WORLD. I don't know how you do everything you do, but I am in constant awe of you.

To my PAs, Sam and Mikala, you both have worked so hard to make each and every one of my books shine and I appreciate you both so much.

To my early readers, thank you for giving my first dark romance a chance and for your support in sharing this novella.

The Fate of Azala Series

One Hollow Love

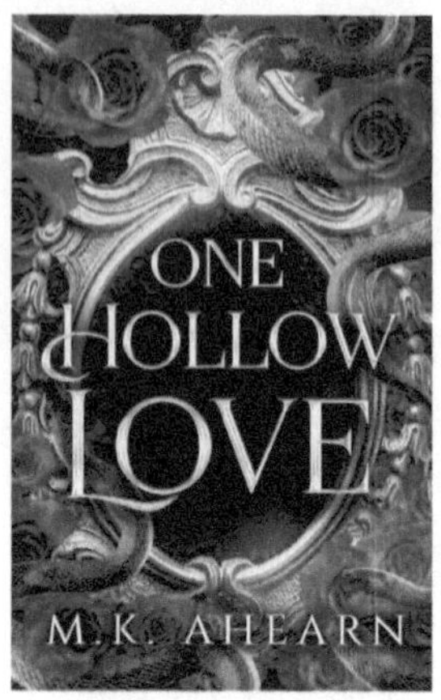

The Elemental Arrangement Series

Aftermath

ABOUT THE AUTHOR

MK Ahearn grew up in Massachusetts as one of three sisters. She now lives in Maryland with her husband, son, and their four cats. She received her bachelor of arts in international relations and a master of professional studies in homeland security. When not writing or studying she can be found planning her next travel adventure.